CRATER LAKE

Jennifer Killick was mentored by the Golden Egg Academy and carried out a Creative Writing MA at Brunel University, which is where she got the idea for her first book, *Alex Sparrow and the Really Big Stink*. Jennifer lives in Uxbridge in a house full of animals and children.

Other books by Jennifer Killick
from Firefly Press:

Alex Sparrow and the Really Big Stink
Alex Sparrow and the Furry Fury
Alex Sparrow and the Zumbie Apocalypse

Mo Lottie and the Junkers
Crater Lake: Evolution

CRATER LAKE

by Jennifer Killick

Firefly

First published in 2020
by Firefly Press
25 Gabalfa Road, Llandaff North, Cardiff, CF14 2JJ
www.fireflypress.co.uk

A CIP catalogue record of this book is available from
the British Library.

9

Print ISBN 978-1-913102-20-3
Ebook ISBN 978-1-913102-21-0

This book has been published with the support of the
Welsh Books Council.

Typeset by: Elaine Sharples

Printed by CPI Group (UK) Ltd, Croydon, Surrey, CRO 4YY

Contents

1
Geek, Robot, Overlord

'Anyone want to Geek, Robot, Overlord for the last cookie?' I say, as the coach takes a sharp right on to a country lane.

'But if you win, you'll give it to Katja.' Big Mak looks round from the seat in front. 'If Kat wins, she'll give it to you; if I win, Chets will whinge at me until I give it to him...'

'And anyway, Chetan's already eaten it.' Katja peeps at us over the top of her seat. 'Haven't you, Chets?'

'Why do you assume I've eaten it?' says Chets.

I look at him and laugh. 'You've got the crumbs of guilt around your mouth, mate.'

I pretend not to notice as Chetan makes out he's cleaning off the bits of cookie while actually pushing them into his mouth.

'Of course Chubby Chets ate the last cookie,' Trent shouts from the back seat. He always ruins everything. 'Geek, Robot, Overlord. Best of three,' he says to his mates. 'Loser has to share a room with Fangs and probably won't make it through the night. Who wants to play?'

Everyone on the back seat laughs like Trent is the funniest guy in the world. I've known him since Reception and I can tell you, legit, he isn't. And not just because most of his dumb jokes are about me. He just all round sucks.

'If anyone gets to share a room with Lance, it should be me,' Chets pipes up, totally missing the point. 'I'm his best friend.'

'Chubby and Fangy share a room, Chubby gobbles up Fangy's tomb.' Trent falls over the back of the seat in front, laughing at his own joke-slash-poem. I like to give respect where it's earned but, let's face it, not that clever or funny.

'Wow – Trent made a rhyme,' I say, rolling my eyes at his smug face. 'Say what you want about me, but leave Chetan out of it.'

'That's OK, Lance – I can take a joke.' Chets is kneeling on his seat, facing the back of the coach. Everything about him is neat and sensible, and he has eyes like balls of chocolate – all gooey and sincere.

'Yeah, chill out, Lance,' Trent says, and they go

back to playing Geek, Robot, Overlord, which is the Montmorency Year Six version of Rock, Paper, Scissors. Trent claims he made it up during a wet break back in October, but it was actually me, Chets, Big Mak and Katja's creation. It's been used for making every important decision ever since.

'Overlord enslaves Geek, I win again,' Trent shouts.

Trent almost always plays Overlord, so he's easy to beat. But his mates either haven't realised or don't want to make him mad, so they keep pulling out the Geek. All of them are so predictable.

'Good one, Trent,' Chets calls and turns and sits down again.

'Why do you do that, Chets?'

'Do what?'

'Suck up to Trent. He's not your friend and he never will be. I don't understand why you would even want him to be.'

'Mum says he's a wonderful boy. And as we're both going to Bing Academy, it makes sense for us to stick together.'

'There will be hundreds of people at Bing. You don't need him.'

'Hopefully you'll go up the waiting list really fast, and then you can come to Bing with me.' Chetan smiles at me.

'Mate, it's a long list. It might take ages to get in.' That's what I say to Chets, but inside I know I'm never getting in. I didn't take the entrance test and I'm not on the waiting list. I can't tell Chets that, though.

'And when you arrive, you'll have Trent and me to show you around.'

The clouds are extra fluffy in Chets' world.

'Year Six – I want everyone to quieten down and face the front.'

Miss Hoche, the assistant head, stands up at the front of the coach, trying not to fall as it bumps up the country road. I always think saying her name sounds like you're trying to cough up something nasty, which works because it's how she makes me feel.

'I'm now going to provide you with some information,' she says, pronouncing the long words especially slowly and clearly for those of us who are too dumb to understand people speaking at normal speed – aka me, or so she thinks.

'This information is of the greatest importance

4

for ensuring you have a safe and productive trip. Some of you…' (she looks at me) '…should be paying particular attention to the information about the rules.'

Damn, if she says 'information' one more time…

'There will be stickers presented to the children who demonstrate exemplary behaviour.' She beams at Trent, Adrianne and Chets. 'And punishments for those who let the rest of the class down by being disruptive.' I'll give you one guess who she looks at when she says that.

She opens a leaflet and starts to read. 'Crater Lake is a new and innovative activity centre, designed with the needs and safety of your children in mind to provide an unforgettable learning experience.' She looks up. 'We're actually the first school to be trying out this centre, so we're extremely fortunate.'

'My mum is a parent governor,' Trent says, loud enough so I will hear, 'and she told me we're stuck going to Crater Lake because some people's scummy parents refused to pay for the good activity centres.' More laughing from the jerks at the back.

'The centre was built deep in rural Sussex, in a crater thought to have been formed when a meteor hit the earth's surface hundreds of years ago,' Hoche continues.

'A meteor from space, Miss?' someone asks.

'Yes, of course. Where else would a meteor come from?'

'A meaty rowing boat,' Big Mak whispers from the seat in front of me and we crack up.

Miss Hoche glares at us.

'The deepest part of the crater is home to Crater Lake itself, as the River Whist, which used to run past the site, took a detour many years ago and now feeds into the crater. The lake is the ideal arena for many of our daring water activities, such as swimming, canoeing and our epic game, "The Last Man Standing".'

'So sexist,' Adrianne sighs. Adrianne is head girl, super-smart and looks kind of like an angry sparrow. You wouldn't mess with her. If anyone in our class is going to win a game called Last Man Standing, I'd bet everything I own that it would be Adrianne.

'Other outdoor activities include the climbing wall, obstacle course and the Leap of Faith.'

'I don't like the sound of that,' Chets says.

'Chets,' I say, putting my hand on his arm for added reassurance. 'They're not going to let us do anything even slightly dangerous.'

'That's true,' Katja nods. 'There are laws.'

'I heard you have to jump over a ravine filled with starving crocodiles,' Big Mak says. Chets looks horrified.

'The dormitories, chill-out zone…' (the whole class rolls their eyes) '…dining hall and bathrooms are located in the main building, which is built on a rise in the crater.' At this point I start to slip into a coma. Miss Hoche always says at least a hundred more things than are necessary.

'Do I have your attention, Lance Sparshott?' She's suddenly standing right in front of my seat.

'Yes, Miss.'

She leans in way too close to my face. I'm in the window seat, so Chets has to squash himself into the back of his seat to avoid any uncomfortable physical contact. Her breath smells like coffee and muddy dog.

'You're lucky to be on this trip. If there was any way I could prove what we both know you did at the beginning of the year, you would have been excluded. If you take even the smallest step out of line, you'll be done, and there will be a black mark on your school record before you've even started at Latham High.'

She withdraws from mine and Chets' seating area, like a swamp monster oozing back into its pit, and starts walking towards the front of the coach again. Chets is frozen, burrowed so far into the padding of the seat that if his skin was some weird purple and blue triangular print, he'd be totally camouflaged.

'Bit too close for you?' I say.

'No words,' he mutters, without blinking.

Katja giggles, and Big Mak coughs to cover a snort of laughter.

'Something funny?' Miss Hoche spins round.

We all look at the floor.

'Stickers for everyone for excellent listening,' Miss Hoche says. 'Except Lance, Maksym and Katja.'

Yeah, no listening stickers for us – that punishment really burns.

'The rules of Crater Lake are as follows.' She nearly falls as she wobbles back to her seat where she left the leaflet. Katja and Big Mak are desperately trying not to laugh. Chets is motionless. Probably still in shock.

'Six children – either boys or girls, not both – to a room…'

(Please don't say what I know you're going to say, Hoche).

'Except for Lance, who has to have his own room due to personal issues.'

Whispers and sniggers all around. I hate her.

'Nobody is to enter a dormitory other than their own. You must remain in your rooms throughout the night. Mr Tomkins, Miss Rani and myself will be watching at all times.' She pauses to stare around at all of us, just to remind us how good she is at watching.

'Never wander the site alone,' she continues. 'You must always be accompanied by a member of staff.'

Sucking the fun right out of everything as usual.

'You must follow any and all instructions given to you by a member of staff. This is for your own safety.'

Chets nods enthusiastically.

'And of course – have fun! Your experience at Crater Lake is going to be one you'll remember for the rest of your lives.'

9

She smiles – I think she's waiting for us to clap or something. There's an awkward moment of silence and then stuff gets crazy.

The coach lurches at the same time as the driver shouts and the brakes screech. We all fall forward, smacking our heads on the seats in front. Miss Hoche stacks it full force and rolls around on the floor. Bags, books and sandwiches fly through the air, landing in sticky piles. Atul's unicorn pillow gets covered in mayonnaise. One of Jordan's limited-edition WWE wrestling cards flies out of an open window and flutters away to freedom. 'May the force be with you, John Cena,' I call as it disappears into the trees. A slice of ham catches in Chets' hair, which is especially bad cos he's a vegetarian. It's chaos.

The coach skids to a stop.

'What happened?' Hoche gasps at the driver.

'There's someone in the road.'

Of course, everyone rushes forward, trying to see out of the front window.

'Everybody back to your seats!' Hoche screams above the noise, and she and the other teachers form a human barricade at the front of the coach.

'I'll call an ambulance,' the driver says, grabbing his mobile and stabbing at the buttons. (It's one of those old-fashioned ones without a touch screen you hardly see anymore.) 'Has anyone got a signal? I have no signal!'

The teachers all check their phones and shake their heads.

'Why do we need an ambulance?' Chets says. 'Nobody seems hurt.'

'I don't think it's for us,' I say, angling my head as far out of the crack of open window as I can. 'I think it's for whoever's outside.'

All I can see is the empty road, and nothing but trees for miles around. I press my face to the glass again, so hot it almost burns my skin, at the same time as a bloody hand thumps against the window from the other side.

2
Zombie

'Argh!' I jump backwards into Chets as Katja screams.

There is a man outside. He's wearing a torn polo shirt with the Crater Lake logo on it. His jeans are dirty and shredded. He's bleeding from at least six different places that I can see, the worst injury being a gash across the side of his head. As I watch, a fresh gush of blood trickles quickly down his face. I've witnessed a lot of nasty stuff in my life, but I've never seen something bleed like that before.

Aside from the blood, the bruises, and the clothes that look like they've been lawn-mowered, the most horrible thing about him is his eyes. They're bright red and swollen, and the skin around them is purpley-black. It sags off his face like a half-deflated bouncy castle from some kind of sick Halloween party. The guy is messed up.

'Zombie!' Chets shouts and the chaos of the

crash that almost happened seems like a flipping tea party compared to what happens next.

Half the class screams and panics, trying to grab their most precious possessions, before realising all they have with them is junk because it's a school trip and you aren't allowed to bring your decent stuff, and hiding under their seats instead. The other half of the class bulldoze towards my bit of window in excitement, desperately trying to see the Crater Lake zombie before the teachers pull us away for our own 'protection', like they'd be able to save us from a zombie apocalypse.

'I don't think he's a zombie,' I say. 'If he was a zombie, he would have eaten people, and there are no bits of intestines between his teeth.'

'You're right, Lance,' Katja says. 'He actually has very nice teeth. I think he's just hurt. Maybe we ran him over.'

'I didn't feel us hit anything, and I reckon he'd be way more broken if we had,' says Big Mak. 'This coach must weigh at least ten tonnes. If we'd hit him, he'd be splattered all over the floor.'

'Someone really ought to go and help him.' Adrianne pushes through the kids towards the teachers. 'That man needs first aid, urgently.'

'Dale. His name's Dale,' Katja says.

'I always knew Katja was a witch,' Trent whoops. 'She has those creepy eyes that can obviously see in the dark. And now we know she can read minds.'

'Shut-up, Trent, you idiot.' I turn on him, wanting so much to punch him in his nasty mouth. 'Katja's not a witch. It says Dale on his name badge.'

At last, the teachers get the balls to open the coach door and go outside. Dale is staggering around, his eyes half closed. He's practically unconscious when Mr Tomkins approaches him.

'Dale? Are you OK, mate?'

Obviously Dale is not OK, but Mr Tomkins is an alright guy, so I'll let it pass.

Dale doesn't respond.

'Dale? Why don't you come to the side of the road? We can lay you down while we get help.'

'NO!' Dale suddenly comes to life. 'Need water!'

'Can someone pass me some water for him?' Mr Tomkins calls.

'Bears!' Dale shouts, grabbing Mr Tomkins with his crusty hands. He smears blood and some kind of green mush all over the pink T-shirt Mr Tomkins wears for every mufti school event cos he thinks it's really trendy.

'Calm down, Dale. You're hurt, you've had a bump on the head.'

'Get on the coach, turn around. Get us away!' Dale is ranting and swaying. 'They'll get us if we stay here. They'll get us all.'

Finally he loses his battle with sanity-slash-consciousness and keels over in the road, dropping like Santa's sack at the end of his Christmas Eve deliveries. Miss Rani runs out with a towel to put under his head. He flaps his hands around weakly and looks like he might try to get up, but at last he goes limp and still.

'Like a rotting goldfish,' I say, as Mr Tomkins starts to cover him with a blanket.

'OMG, he's dead!' Atul shouts.

'I don't think he's dead. Probably just passed out from blood loss or shock.' Big Mak seems strangely knowledgeable about life-threatening injuries.

'Or he has concussion,' says Adrianne.

'I hope he's not dead,' Katja says, rubbing the grimy window with her sleeve to try and see more clearly. 'No, look. Mr Tomkins hasn't covered his head. They always put the blanket over the face if they're dead.'

'If he isn't dead,' I say, 'he soon will be with that blanket over him. It's about a million degrees today. Poor guy.'

We watch as the adults, who supposedly know exactly what they're doing in situations like this, have a worried chat amongst themselves. Finally, Hoche gets back on the coach.

'Right, children – it's your lucky day. You get to start your Crater Lake adventure early!'

'Is the dead guy part of the experience?' Big Mak asks.

'Don't be ridiculous, Maksym. The chap outside has just had a bit of a bump on the head, so he's having a lie down while he waits for some medical attention. He's perfectly fine.'

We look through the blood-smeared window at half-dead zombie, Dale. Miss Hoche really does talk a load of garbage.

'The driver is going to wait with him, and we're going the rest of the way to the activity centre on foot. With the luggage. It will be like a cross-country hike.'

Of course everyone groans. It's too hot to move, let alone drag our massive bags down a gravelly road.

Ten minutes later, we're walking down the road in twos, loaded down with masses of stuff.

'See you in a few days,' Miss Hoche calls to the driver. 'We'll call for help as soon as we get to a landline.'

'Have fun, kids,' the driver nods to us, sweat dripping off his nose.

'Eyes forward, please, children,' Hoche says as we pass not-dead Dale and his blood-spattered section of the road. 'Aren't we fortunate to be surrounded by such beautiful countryside, and on such a lovely day.'

'Not such a lovely day for Dale.' Katja looks at him sadly.

'How far do you think it is?' Chets asks, looking around nervously. 'Do you think there are bandits in the woods?'

Big Mak, Katja and I burst out laughing.

'What is it? What's funny?'

'Only you would use the word "bandits", Chets,' Mak says.

'I don't think there are any bandits outside of

the Wild Wild West,' I say, pushing the strap on my backpack further up my shoulder cos it's starting to dig in.

'Well, someone attacked that guy,' Chets says.

'And did you hear what he was saying to Mr Tomkins?' says Katja. 'All that stuff about having to turn back or they'll get us all.'

'He might have been hallucinating – heat exhaustion or the bang on the head.' Big Mak is the only one of us apparently not struggling with his bags. I swear he's part giant.

'Maybe he was mugged,' Katja says.

'I don't think so. Muggers lurk in dark alleys or park bushes. They don't hang out in the woods. They have to stay near the fried-chicken shops because that's where they get their food.'

Chets says this with a completely straight face. This is why we love him.

We laugh so hard.

'So we've ruled out zombies and muggers,' I say. 'What's left? Badgers with a vendetta?'

'Orcs,' says Mak.

'Tree monsters,' says Katja.

'Alien body-snatchers,' I joke and even Chets laughs this time. 'You were probably right the first time, Chets. It'll be those pesky bandits. We'd better get to this cruddy activity centre and call the sheriff.'

As we trudge round the corner I see the looming gates of Crater Lake, starkly black against the clear blue sky.

3
Entering the Crater

By the time we reach the gate, we're the kind of hot that's so intense you can't even remember what cold feels like. We dump our bags on the ground while Hoche looks for a way in. On either side of the gate is a spike-topped fence that stretches through the woods for as far as I can see. And on the other side of the gate there is only the dusty road and a butt-load more trees.

'Shouldn't someone be here to open the gate?' Mr Tomkins asks. 'I thought they were expecting us.'

Now that the moment of shock and horror is over, I can tell he's seriously triggered about his favourite T-shirt.

'I think it's fantastic that they take security so seriously. The children are going to be completely safe here,' Hoche says.

'She'll probably give them a sticker for that,' I say, and the others laugh.

Without warning, the gates shudder and start to open.

'Like magic,' Hoche beams.

'There are cameras, Miss,' Adrianne says, pointing to the top of the gateposts.

'Not Hogwarts, though, is it?' Katja whispers.

'More like Arkham Asylum,' I say, as the gates rattle to a stop and the space between them seems to beckon us in a creepily silent way.

'Where actually is the centre?' Mr Tomkins says, looking down the winding road that disappears over the horizon. 'Is it much further? It looks like miles.'

'He wants to get his T-shirt in the wash,' I say.

'Before that stain dries in,' Katja giggles.

'I'm sure it's not much further!' Hoche grabs the handle of her wheelie case. 'Come on – let's sing some motivational songs to make the walk more pleasant.'

We all groan. Our mouths are rabbit-poo dry and the last thing we want to do is sing. Miss Hoche struts ahead anyway, pulling her case, which is cream-coloured with sparkly bits on it, the same as her jacket (yes, she's wearing a flipping jacket) and shoes. Nobody has ever seen

Miss Hoche wearing shoes that aren't high heels. She wears them in the snow. She wears them on Sports Day. And apparently she wears them to activity centres in the middle of nowhere. William Breeming from Year Four swears he saw her when he was on holiday in Switzerland, and that she was wearing high heels while skiing. Nobody really believes that he saw her, because we all know that teachers don't do anything with their lives outside of school, but the thought of her wearing heels on skis is not that much of a stretch.

So we walk for ages, until finally the road starts to dip downwards and we get our first proper view of Crater Lake.

The crater is bigger than I thought – it's like a bowl set into the ground and it's roomy enough to be the next Jurassic Park. A river wiggles back and forth down the least steep side and flows into the lake at the bottom. A wooden pier thing stretches from a hut at the edge of the lake into the middle, and there are canoes lined up against it. Halfway up the steeper side is a large building that looks kind of like a school, or a prison, although those are pretty much the same thing. There's a flat, grassy area next to the building and I can see a climbing wall at one end and the obstacle course running across it. Overall it looks like either a completely awesomely fun place, or the perfect location for a Goosebumps book.

'Do you think there are snakes?' Chets asks, edging forward to peer down the slope of the crater. His foot catches on a mound of moss and he almost tumbles down the hill.

'Oh, man!'

Chets is not a fan of nature.

'Maybe little ones,' I say. 'Nothing poisonous.'

'I wish we were sharing a room.'

I should tell you about how me and Chets became friends. Chets joined halfway through year one, when all the friendship groups were basically formed. Nobody made much of an effort with Chets. He wore his uniform too neatly and looked like a lost baby owl. I kind of felt sorry for him, but I had my own troubles to deal with. Anyway, he was standing on his own one lunchtime when a wasp landed on his ear. Everyone else screamed and laughed and ran to a safe distance, but he just stood there. The fear on his face was like nothing I'd ever seen before. He was more scared in that moment than I'd ever been of anything in my life, and I couldn't stand it. I ran over and flicked the wasp away. I saved Chets and got stung in the process. It's pretty much been like that ever since.

One thing I can't do for Chets, as Hoche so unkindly reminded everyone, is share a room. I've never had a sleepover at my house, and I've never slept over at anyone else's, because … reasons. The word at school is it's because I'm a vampire, and that wasn't really helped by the fact that when some of my teeth grew in, they looked sort of pointy. They're rubbed down a lot now, but people don't like to forget that kind of thing. That's why they call me Fangs. But, as I can't tell them the truth, I just suck it up and hope that one day my life will be normal.

So I just say, 'Sorry, Chets.'

We start making our way down the slope towards the building. The air is so thick with heat that we practically have to chew our way through it, and all I can hear is the crunch of our feet on the gravel path.

'It's so quiet,' Katja says.

'Like end-of-the-world quiet,' I agree.

'If it was the end of the world,' Big Mak stops to

take a sip of water, 'do you think Hoche would still be wearing those shoes?'

'Probably,' says Chets.

'Imagine if she put on some trainers,' I say. 'It would be like the first sign of the apocalypse.'

'Mum says presentation is important, and that it's impressive that Miss Hoche sets such a great example for us all,' Chets says.

'Yeah, but your mum also makes you wear a shirt and tie on non-uniform day, when the rest of us are chilling in our jeans,' I say. 'Not sure we should agree with everything she comes out with.'

'True dat,' says Chets, and we all crack up again.

By the time we reach the building's entrance we still haven't seen a single human being.

'Shouldn't there be Crater Lake dudes around, like, doing stuff?' Big Mak says.

Hoche presses a buzzer next to the door. Nothing happens.

'They must be busy getting ready for us,' she says and buzzes again – three loud blasts.

We stare at the frosted glass on the double doors but can't see any movement behind it.

She presses again, holding down the buzzer for a good ten seconds.

Nothing but silence.

A screech and a crackle suddenly splits the air in two and a voice says over some kind of tannoy system: 'Attention, Montmorency pupils and teachers. Welcome to Crater Lake, where adventure awaits. I have released the lock, please push the door and seat yourselves in the waiting area. I will be with you presently to prepare you for a visit that will change you forever.' Another crackle, and the door clicks open.

We sit in the waiting room, which is so new it still smells of paint, and chat amongst ourselves. It's been a weird day so far and something about Crater Lake just feels off.

We expect stuff to happen, for people to come and tell us what's going on, but we're left alone for ages. Adrianne walks over to the other two doors in the room and pulls on the handles, but they're both locked.

At last the door opens and a huge man with a bald head walks into the room. 'Apologies for the delay,' he says, wiping his hands on his trousers. 'Which one of you is Miss Hoche?'

'That would be me,' Hoche jumps up. I can tell she's torn between being annoyed by the wait and wanting to carry on pretending that everything is just fabulous.

'Welcome to Crater Lake,' the man says. 'My name is Digger.' He points to his name badge as if to prove Digger actually is his name, which, to be fair, I'm a bit doubtful about. 'I'm the centre manager here, and, as our very first guests, I wanted to take care of you myself.'

'That's super, Digger.' Hoche pronounces his name as if it tastes disgusting in her mouth. 'There's been an accident just outside your gates. A young chap who works here seems to have had a mishap and is unconscious in the road. Our coach and driver are waiting with him but we have no mobile reception. Could you call an ambulance urgently, please?'

'One of our chaps?' Digger asks, not looking especially concerned.

'His name is Dale,' Adrianne says. 'He's wearing a Crater Lake polo shirt. Have you not noticed he's missing?'

'Ah yes, Dale. We have been looking for him. He's unconscious, you say?'

'Unconscious and bleeding from the head.' Hoche nods.

'Possibly dead,' Chets says.

'Thank you so much for letting me know,' Digger says. And get this – he smiles, really smiles. Me, Chets, Katja and Big Mak raise eyebrows at each other.

'I'll deal with him immediately. Please excuse me for one minute more.'

'Of course,' Hoche says.

Digger goes back through the door, which magically opens for him even though it's stuck tight for all of us.

'Maybe he has super-strength,' I say. 'He walks like a minotaur.'

'Or maybe this is Hogwarts after all,' says Katja.

When he comes back, he and the teachers talk business and so do we. So far this trip has not been what we expected. A lot of seriously weird stuff has gone on and we haven't been even near a rope swing or made to build a replica of the Shard out of lolly sticks. And, apparently, we're not going to be participating in any activities today.

'Children,' Hoche says. 'We've decided that the best thing to do is relax tonight and start fresh in the morning. Once we've unpacked, perhaps you could give us a tour of the centre, Digger?'

'I'm afraid the staff are busy and I'm needed elsewhere. We'll make sure you're fully acquainted with Crater Lake tomorrow. May I show you to your rooms?' Digger says, picking up about ten suitcases and walking through the door without giving her a chance to argue.

As he hoists a backpack over his shoulder, I notice some spatters down the side of his polo shirt.

'Is that blood?' Big Mak asks. 'It looks like blood.'

Unfortunately, Trent is right behind us. 'I thought you vampires only attacked people at night, Sparshott,' he laughs. 'Couldn't wait to sink your fangs in, could you?'

'Lance has been here the whole time, Trent,' Chets says. 'It couldn't have been him.'

'Well, I don't see any other bloodsuckers around here, Chubby.'

Trent and his mates crack up.

'What's all the noise?' Hoche glares over at us.

'Lance and Chetan were just discussing dinner, Miss.' Trent smirks.

'Then I shall have to take a house point from Lance for being rude and disruptive.'

Totally fair.

'Is dinner almost ready to be served, Digger?' she asks the walrus on legs, who is striding ahead.

'Dinner?' He stops for a moment but doesn't turn around. 'Dinner. Yes, dinner will be ready ... soon. The staff have been preparing it.'

'Fabulous. And could I trouble you for something to drink first, please, Digger?' Hoche says. 'We've walked a long way in this heat and the children could really do with some cool water.'

Digger drops the bags he's carrying. His hands fall to his sides. He sort of shivers, which is weird because, like I said, it's extra-hot in here. He seems to take a moment. You'd think she'd asked him to murder a baby swan or something. Then he bends to pick up the bags. 'There are drinking fountains in the communal areas. Please help yourselves.'

He walks us down a wide corridor and stops at the top of a narrow flight of stairs which, unlike the rest of the place, doesn't look newly decorated.

'The single room is down there, for the child with special needs,' Digger says, pointing to a door at the bottom of the stairs that looks suspiciously like it leads to a basement.

'Lance!' Hoche and Trent call at the same time.

A few people snigger. I pick up my bags and push through the class to the stairway.

'Looks like the place where all the bodies are buried,' Chets whispers.

'Perfect for Fangs, then,' Trent says.

'Vampires suck blood from the living, not the dead, idiot,' I say, as I accidentally whack his shoulder with my backpack.

'The room is fully furnished,' Digger says. 'But for significant reasons we had to rechannel resources, so the outside isn't complete.'

'I'm sure it will be adequate for Lance,' Hoche says. 'It's better than he deserves, anyway.'

The rest of the class continue down the corridor, Big Mak, Katja and Chets turning to smile encouragingly at me before they go. I tell myself I'm not that bothered – that I'm OK with being alone. And it's true that the thought of sharing a room with anyone makes me feel sick.

I open the door, half expecting to be ambushed by a killer clown, but the room is boringly normal. I shove my clothes into a drawer, and hide my equipment under the bed, just in case someone decides to have a snoop. Sitting on my bed, on my own in the dead quiet of the centre, a little bit of sadness creeps in. I imagine the others mucking around in their dorms, having fun together. Then I text my mum from the phone I snuck in, knowing it probably won't send because of the no-reception thing, to tell her I'm having a brilliant time.

4
Soup or Blood?

After about thirty minutes I hear voices calling me from outside the door. 'Come on, Lance – we're going to dinner!'

We all walk to the dining hall, which is in the middle of the building – a massive room with high ceilings and wooden floors – kind of like the gym at school. There are long tables with benches on either side and a hatch where the food is served. We grab trays and queue at the hatch, expecting to be greeted by dinner ladies wearing those weird fishing nets over their hair under hats that look like they're made of the same stuff as shower curtains. But there is only one person behind the hatch, and it's Digger.

I'm towards the end of the queue but it soon becomes clear that there is only one choice of food.

'Dinner is served,' Digger says when it's my turn. He dumps a bowl of tomato soup on my tray.

'Err, thanks,' I say and walk to a table to sit with my friends. Everyone looks confused, cos soup isn't generally considered to be a dinner food; it's the food your mum gives you in the winter when you have a cold.

'No wonder we haven't seen anyone other than Digger,' I say. 'They've obviously all been rushing around preparing this delicious feast.'

'I think Digger did this on his own,' Chets whispers, not noticing my sarcasm because he's clearly deeply distressed. Chets is fond of his food.

'Maybe that's what the spatters on his clothes were,' Katja says, stirring the soup around her bowl.

'I know soup, and I know blood,' Mak says. Which seem like two strangely specific and unrelated fields of expertise. 'Those spatters were definitely blood and this is definitely soup.'

'I don't even think it's Heinz.' Chets has tears in his eyes. 'It's one of those supermarket value soups.' None of us are keen.

'Lucky I have a stack of brownies and crisps in my room, then,' I say, giving Chets a nudge. 'We'll meet up after lights out and have a picnic. Or maybe not a picnic because we're not toddlers with teddy bears, but a cooler version of a picnic. A sicknic. But not like vomit sick.'

'Awesome,' Katja says. 'As long as I can sneak out of my room without the other girls telling.'

'I'm in,' says Big Mak.

'But what if we get caught?' Chets says.

'You can always fill yourself up on this tasty tomato soup,' I say. 'Hold on, I'll ask Digger if you can have another bowl.'

Chets looks at his soup. 'Fine, I'll do it,' he says.

As soon as 'dinner' is over, Digger herds us into the lounge area, where there are comfy sofas, board games and a big TV, which is stuck on one channel no matter how hard we try to change it.

'I guess they don't want us watching *World War Z*,' Mak says, as we sit on the wooden floor, hoping it will be a bit cooler than the giant cushions.

'You'd think they'd have air con,' Chets says. 'It's hotter in here than it is outside.'

'I think they do – look at those vents,' I say, pointing up at the ceiling. I slide myself across the floor on my bum so that I'm directly underneath one. 'I guess it's not working,' I say.

'This place gets better and better.' Chets huffs, throwing his cap on the floor. 'I'm sure there must be some kind of legal jurisdiction about imprisoning children in these temperatures.'

'We're not exactly imprisoned,' Katja says. 'We could get out if we really wanted to.'

'We're not allowed, though. I heard Digger telling Miss Hoche to make sure we all stayed here. He said the paint wasn't quite dry in some areas of the centre and he doesn't want us to get dizzy from the fumes.'

Too hot and bored to do anything else, we look up at the TV. There's a show about deadly animals on, and it's talking about wasps.

'Just my luck,' says Chets.

'*There are two main subgroups of wasp...*' the presenter says, '*...social and solitary. Social colonies are started by a queen, who wakes from hibernation when it starts to get warm, builds a small nest and creates a swarm of worker wasps to rapidly expand it.*'

'I wonder what makes the queen so special?' Katja says. 'Is she bigger? Or cleverer?'

'Probably bossier,' Big Mak says. 'That's the way with girls.'

36

Katja thumps him on the arm.

'If the nest is disturbed, the social wasps release a pheromone which drives their fellow wasps into a stinging frenzy. Solitary wasps do not form colonies. But unlike social wasps who use their stings only for defence, solitary wasps hunt using their venom to attack their prey.'

Chets shudders and rubs his ear. 'So there are nice little worker wasps, and nasty big hunter wasps.'

'And all-powerful queen wasps who tell the others what to do.' Hoche is standing behind us. 'So everybody knows their job and does it efficiently. If only our school could be like that.'

She laughs and clacks off in her heels.

'Don't judge me,' I say, 'but for the first time in my life, I feel sorry for Mr Moody.' Mr Moody is our head teacher, and he's kind of nice, actually, especially when you compare him to Hoche. 'She's probably just waiting for an opportunity to get rid of him.'

'Imagine if Hoche was the Head-head,' Katja says.

'She'd be unstoppable.' Mak makes a face.

'She'd be a maniac,' I say.

'At least we're leaving in a couple of weeks. Think of the younger kids.' Katja's eyes widen so you can really see how turquoise they are.

We all look at each other for a moment and I imagine this was what it was like when the people safe on the lifeboats realised that everyone else on the Titanic was going to die.

'May God have mercy on their souls.'

'Some wasps use prey as hosts for their parasitic larvae. Though this is unpleasant for the creatures used as hosts, it is a highly efficient way of ridding the ecosystem of unwanted pests.'

'Does that mean what I think it means?' asks Chets.

'They use the living bodies of other creatures to grow their wasp babies in,' I say.

'That's disgusting.'

'Yeah. Especially if you're one of the unwanted pests.'

'Maybe we could get a wasp to lay her eggs in Trent,' Katja says, looking over to where Trent is refusing to let anyone else play on the football table unless they can name every player in the Arsenal squad from 1968 through to 2020.

'I reckon the wasp babies deserve a nicer home.'

We watch in silence as a bunch of squirming maggots burst their way out of a distressed caterpillar. It's horrific.

'I'm glad I'm not a caterpillar,' Chets says.

We agreed that the others would come to my room at 10.30pm. The teachers would all have had their sneaky glasses of wine and tucked themselves up for the night by then. Honestly, if you were an adult and could go to bed whenever you liked, why would you go as early as you could? Such a waste.

I make sure my stuff is completely out of sight. Chets, Mak and Katja are my best friends, but for some reason I've never been able to bring myself to be straight with them about why I never stay round their houses, and why I never invite them to mine. At first it was just because of Mum, but when my own problems developed, what had seemed embarrassing and tough before became a thousand times worse. I was ashamed, I guess, so I kept it secret. And now it feels too late to tell them.

Ten-thirty comes and nobody knocks. I wait another ten minutes, then put my ear to the door. All I hear is silence.

I've never been able to stand waiting for things

to happen, so it isn't hard to make the decision to find out what's going on.

I open my door as quietly as possible and creep up the stairs. You'd think it would have cooled down a bit, what with the sun having set, but if anything it feels hotter than it did during the day. I don't bother putting my shoes on – I'll be quieter in my bare feet anyway. I move quickly but carefully up the corridor towards the dorm rooms. If a teacher was to come along there would be nowhere to hide and I really can't afford to get in any more trouble with Hoche. She's had it in for me since the incident with Trent back at the start of Year Six. She's decided I was responsible, and that's all that matters to her.

Chets and Mak told me their dorm room was first on the left in the main corridor, but when I reach it, I listen at the door, just in case. I can hear whispered voices, and when the handle suddenly turns I jump back, not knowing who to expect. But the door doesn't open. Someone on the inside tries the handle again and rattles the door in the frame.

There's a key in the lock and it occurs to me that somebody has locked them in. I have a moment to make a decision. I turn the key and unlock the door.

'What the hell?' Big Mak is standing in the doorway with Chets right behind him. 'Did you lock us in?'

'Course not. You guys never showed, so I came to look for you and saw that your door was locked.'

'Maybe it was that jerk, Trent,' Mak whispers.

'I don't think it would have been Trent,' Chets whispers back. 'Maybe it was the same person who trapped Trent in the toilets at the start of the year. You know, the thing you got the blame for, Lance.'

'Maybe,' I say. 'Is Trent in a different dorm?'

'Yeah, he's next door, thank God,' says Mak. 'And Katja's room is the one opposite.'

'Is everyone else in your dorm asleep?'

'We think so.'

'Then let's try Katja's door,' I say.

We check both ways as though we're about to cross the road, though I don't really know why we bother cos if anyone comes, we're absolutely sunk. I pull down the handle to Katja's room and gently push the door. It's locked.

'This is messed up,' I whisper, turning the key

and pushing the door open. At least, because everything here is new, there aren't any creaks to give us away.

'Lance,' Katja says when she sees us. 'Someone locked us in.'

Adrianne and some of the other girls are standing behind her. 'Why would someone lock us in? It's against all the fire regulations.'

'It must have been Trent,' Big Mak says. 'Our room was locked, too.'

'But your room wasn't locked?' Adrianne asks me.

'No, mine was open. Otherwise you'd all still be locked in.'

'Then I don't think it was Trent. If he was going to lock anyone in, it would have been Lance. Especially after the incident...'

'At the beginning of Year Six,' I finish for her.

'Ade is right,' Katja says. 'But there's one way to find out for sure.'

'We try Trent's door,' I say.

'Everyone else, stay here,' Adrianne says to the rest of the girls from their dorm. 'If we all go, we'll make too much noise. We'll report back in five.'

The girls do as they're told and go sit on their

beds. I have to hand it to Adrianne; she gets all the respect. She's the type of person you want on your team.

Me, Big Mak, Chets, Katja and Adrianne walk up the corridor to the next door on the boys' side. I feel less worried about getting in trouble now that Adrianne is with us as I know she can talk us out of it – even the teachers do as she says.

When we get to Trent's door we hear a murmur of noise coming from inside.

'They're awake, then,' Chets says.

'Obviously.' I can't see Adrianne rolling her eyes cos it's too dark, but I can practically hear it. Chets has that effect on people.

'So what do we do?' I say, knowing that Trent is waiting for an opportunity to get me into serious trouble.

'I'm going to confront them,' Adrianne says. 'Then we can get this sorted and get back to our rooms.' She turns the door handle.

'Who's there?' a voice calls from inside. 'If that's you, Fangs, I'm going to tell Miss Hoche right now. And you'll get your butt kicked out of school and into one of those special prisons for council-estate kids.'

The door doesn't open.

'It's locked, too,' Adrianne says. 'So it can't have been Trent.'

'Quick – someone's locking us in,' Trent shouts from the other side of the door and we hear footsteps thudding towards it.

'It's me, Adrianne,' she says, loud enough to be heard through the wood. 'And we're not locking you in, we're letting you out.'

'Do we have to?' I say.

Adrianne turns the key, opens the door and barges into the brightly lit room. We follow behind.

'What the hell are you all doing here?' Trent says. 'Not you, Adrianne, you're allowed. But you others – you're not welcome in this room.'

There are six boys in Trent's room, including him, and they're all awake. There are cans of coke and sweet wrappers all over the floor.

'Ah, a sicknic,' I say, and Chets nods and looks hungrily at the sweets.

'Just shut up a minute, Trent,' Adrianne says. 'We have a problem and we need to work together.'

'What problem? Did Chubby and Fangy wet their beds?'

'Somebody has locked all of us in our rooms,' Adrianne says. 'Except Lance.'

'Then it must have been him,' Trent says. 'We all know he has previous when it comes to false imprisonment.'

'It wasn't Lance,' Katja says.

'You would say that, witch-eyes. Everyone knows you want to be his girlfriend.'

'Why do you always have to be such a jerk, Trent?' I say, angry now because Katja is the sweetest person in the world and doesn't deserve to be spoken to like that.

'Trent, it wasn't Lance, I swear,' says Chets. 'We were supposed to be meeting him – he was the one who let us out.'

'Lance's room is rather out of the way,' Adrianne says. 'Maybe whoever locked ours forgot that he was down there.'

'Well, if it wasn't Fangface, who was it?' Trent looks around at all of us. 'The teachers?'

'I don't think so,' Adrianne says. 'They can be annoying but they wouldn't do something so dangerous. If there was a fire, we'd be trapped, and then they'd get sacked for negligence. It doesn't make sense for it to be them.'

'Then it must have been someone from the centre,' Trent says.

We all look at each other. As much as I hate to agree with Trent about anything… 'There has been a lot of weird stuff going on here,' I say.

'Digger was covered in blood,' Big Mak says.

'He was hardly covered, but yes, it did look suspicious.' Adrianne bites her lip.

'That poor guy Dale told us not to come here. He said they'd get us all.' Katja tucks her hair behind her ear.

'And, in case you all didn't notice, HE WAS COVERED IN BLOOD,' Mak says.

I ask the question that all of us have in our heads. 'So are we saying that it might have been Digger who attacked Dale?'

'And what about the rest of the staff? Where are they?' Adrianne asks.

'Is Digger some kind of psycho serial killer?' Trent looks excited at the prospect.

'He did feed us tomato soup for dinner,' Chets says.

'Well, that settles it, then,' I say. 'Something's got to be done.'

'Our first step has to be to tell a teacher,' says Adrianne.

'You should definitely do that – they'll believe you.' I hate to think of the response I'd get if I knocked on Hoche's door to tell her there's a mass murderer running around Crater Lake.

'I should do it. I'm head boy,' Trent says, in a way that provides a perfect example of why he should never have been made head boy.

'We'll go together,' Adrianne says. 'You guys wait here.'

'Adrianne?' I say.

'Yes, Lance?'

'Check if she's wearing those dumb shoes with her pyjamas.'

Adrianne and Trent set off noisily down the corridor. Adrianne is light on her feet, but Trent has the stealth of a zombie elephant. The teachers' rooms are just around the corner.

The rest of us stand around awkwardly in the dorm. My group and Trent's group don't usually hang out, so we don't have much to say. Chets eyes up the pack of sweets and Katja reties her ponytail. Big Mak looks like he's meditating or something.

'I'm going to try the other girls' dorm room door,' I say. I can't stand doing nothing.

'On your own?' Chets says, through a mouthful of chewy sweet.

'I'll just be a sec.' I tiptoe across the corridor and try the handle of the final dorm. Unsurprisingly, it's locked. When I turn the key and peep in, I can see all the girls asleep in their beds. Not wanting to look like a creepy stalker, I quickly back out but manage to walk smack into the door. One of the girls, I think Atul, sits up in her bed.

'Sorry to wake you up, Atul,' I say. 'Despite what this looks like, I was not watching you sleep.'

Atul's on a bottom bunk. She doesn't say anything, just swings her legs around and stands up.

'There's all kinds of stuff going on,' I say. 'Someone – maybe Digger – has been locking us all in our rooms.'

Atul walks towards me, still not saying anything. It's dark so I can't see her clearly, but her silence is making me uncomfortable. I'm worried she's going to sucker punch me in the face or something. I back out of the room.

'So I was just checking if you guys were OK, cos, you know, there might be a maniac on the loose.'

I'm in the corridor now, and Atul is still calmly

walking towards me. Finally, she steps into the light.

'Argh!' I shout, cos I can see her eyes, and they are another world of crazy. 'What the hell, Atul? What's the matter with you?'

She says nothing, just carries on walking out of the room. All I can look at is her eyes. The parts of them that are usually ... brown? Are Atul's eyes brown? I think they're usually brown. Anyway, the coloured part and the pupil are all one colour – black with a kind of metallic blue sheen. But they're not smooth and shiny like eyes usually are – they have a strange texture, like the speaker part on headphones. I wonder for a second if Atul has some kind of eye condition that means she has to wear funny contact lenses at night, but something tells me there's more to it than that. She keeps coming, not fast or slow, but purposefully, if that's a word. I think she's going to grab me, or push me, but she just walks straight past me and heads down the corridor like she's got somewhere to be.

'Miss Hoche's room is locked,' Adrianne says as she and Trent return from their recon mission. 'So is Mr Tomkins' and Miss Rani's.'

'Should we wake them up?'

'Did you see that?' I say. 'Did you see Atul?'

'She's asleep, isn't she?' Adrianne says.

'No, no.' I shake my head. 'She's awake and suffering from a major case of crazy eye.'

'What do you mean? Where is she?' Adrianne turns round, but Atul has already disappeared down the corridor.

'She woke up. And there was something the matter with her. Her eyes were all buggy and she acted as if I didn't exist. Like a sleepwalking wasp person.' I know I sound insane.

'This has all been you, hasn't it, Fangs?' Trent looks angry and happy at the same time. Being offensive and ripping people apart are his favourite things, after all. 'You set this whole thing up to prank us.'

'I did not,' I say. 'Whatever this is, it's way bigger than anything I could pull off.'

'Liar,' Trent shouts, and shoves me into the wall.

'Lance isn't a liar.' Chets comes running from the dorm room, shoving handfuls of sweets into his pocket. 'He always tells the truth.'

As much as I appreciate Chets sticking up for me, I feel a bit guilty because technically I don't always tell the truth.

'If he says Atul had buggy eyes then she did,' Chets says.

'Find her and prove it then,' says Trent.

The noise from our argument has woken the other girls from Atul's dorm. Over Trent's shoulder, I see them sit up, swing their legs round and get out of bed, at exactly the same time. And I'm kind of happy and scared simultaneously cos I know everyone is going to believe what I've been saying about Atul, but also there are now six bug-eyed girls zombing around the centre.

'What the hell?' Adrianne says. I've never heard her swear before. She flattens herself against the wall next to me. Chets' mouth drops open and a pink chewed-up blob of sweet falls out on to the floor.

'What's wrong with you freaks now?' Trent glares at us just as Katja and Big Mak come into the corridor with the rest of the boys from Trent's room.

Adrianne grabs Trent's shoulders and turns him around to face Lily, Simran, Tallulah, Midge and Ela as they emerge from the dark room and walk in single file down the corridor.

'What the heck is wrong with their eyes?' Trent spits as he talks.

'Like I said, they've gone buggy,' I say.

'Their irises and pupils are like wasps' eyes,' Adrianne says. Irises – that's what the coloured bits are called. I knew that.

'What are they doing?' Trent says.

'Why don't we just ask them.' Katja runs up behind Ela and taps her shoulder. 'Hey, Ela – are you OK?'

Ela completely ignores her.

'Where are you going?' asks Katja, walking alongside her. 'What are you doing?'

Ela turns her head to look at Katja with her insect eyes, and says one word only: 'Work.' Then she turns her head again and follows the others.

'Did she say "work"?' Adrianne asks, as Katja jogs back to where we're still standing, glued to the spot.

Katja nods.

'Well, this situation seems to be escalating quickly,' I say.

'We need a crisis meeting – to discuss what we know and what we need to know,' Mak says. 'We need a plan.'

'I think we'd better wake the teachers,' Adrianne says, turning towards their rooms.

'Wait!' I say. 'Whatever happened to the girls

happened to them while they were asleep. The teachers are asleep – what if they've gone buggy too? What if whoever locked us in our rooms wanted this to happen? We need to be prepared.'

'What will we do without the teachers to help? We'll be alone and in danger!' Chets says. 'We're just kids – we don't know how to deal with a situation like this.'

'Just calm down, Chetan. Look, the worst-case scenario is that the teachers have also, you know, bugged out,' Adrianne says. 'Although not ideal, it isn't the end of the world. They're not harmful, are they? Just aesthetically peculiar and focused on some job they have to do.'

'That's true,' I say. 'And "just kids" is a bunch of trash that adults spout to make us think we can't manage without them. It's all about keeping themselves at the top of the chain, Chets. We're actually faster, braver and smarter than they are, especially in situations like this.'

'Well, some of us are,' Mak says, wiggling his eyebrows at Trent.

'We'll be fine if we think logically,' says Adrianne.

'And stick together.' Katja puts her arm through Chets'. She's always kind like that.

'So we'll go, as a group, to the teachers' rooms and be ready for whatever is waiting for us. Agreed?' I look round at the others.

Chets, Mak, Katja and Adrianne nod. Trent and the others huff and look away but don't argue so I'm taking that as agreement.

As a unit, we move down the corridor towards the teachers' rooms. Our first stop is Mr Tomkins – he's the nicest so it'll ease us in gently. I unlock his door, think about entering, but decide to knock loudly instead.

'Mr Tomkins?' Adrianne calls. 'We're sorry to disturb you, but we appear to have a situation on our hands.'

I raise my knuckles to knock again, but I hear movement in the room, so I take a step back and watch as the door handle moves downward and the door swings slowly open.

'Oh dear,' Katja says, as Mr Tomkins walks towards us, his man bun wonky and his eyes extremely buggy.

Big Mak, who is Mr Tomkins' favourite and almost as tall as him, grabs Tomkins' arm and shakes him. 'We need your help, Mr Tomkins.'

Mr Tomkins gently but firmly removes Mak's

hand and walks past us down the corridor. 'Work,' he says.

'Someone should follow,' I say. 'We need to know where they're going.'

'Don't look at me,' Trent says. 'I'm too young to die.'

'How team-spirited of you, Trent,' Adrianne says. 'I'll go.'

'I'll go with you,' says Big Mak.

'Report back to Trent's dorm in ten minutes?' I say.

'Roger that.' Big Mak smiles, and he and Adrianne run after Mr Tomkins.

'I think Maksym has a crush,' Katja whispers to me. Honestly, girls do think about the strangest things – I can't believe that Mak would potentially jeopardise a scouting mission with flirting.

'Miss Rani next,' I say and we knock on her door.

'Miss Rani?' I call, but there's no reply.

'We'll have to go in,' Katja says.

'You'd better go, then. I don't feel comfortable seeing Miss Rani in her night clothes.'

Katja takes a deep breath, opens the door and goes into the room.

'Miss Rani? Wake up, please.' In the dim light I see her gently shake the shape nestled under a sheet on the bed. Then she gasps and runs back out. 'Abort,' she says. 'She's one of them.'

Miss Rani does the same thing as all the other bugs. For a situation that had been shocking ten minutes earlier, I was finding myself growing rather bored of all the stare-y walking.

On to Hoche. My arch-nemesis.

We move along the hall to Hoche's room, expecting a repetition of the knock, wait, be confronted by a bug-eyed space-cadet sequence.

'Hoche's door isn't locked,' I say. In fact it's wide open.

'But it was a few minutes ago – Adrianne said so.' Katja looks at me nervously. We both peer into the room. Everything's where it should be, except for Hoche. Hoche is gone.

5
Preparing for Action

'This is new,' I say.

'Do you think she's gone to get help?' Katja looks around the empty room.

'Maybe,' I say, but the twisting in my gut says different.

'Oh my God,' Katja says, as she's looking under the bed.

'What? What's down there?' I'm expecting horror – Dale's dead body, Hoche hiding with her claws out, a cauldron full of tomato soup.

'Look at all her shoes!' Katja says. 'Six pairs of heels for three days at an activity centre. I don't know if that's stupid or impressive.'

The sound of the speaker system squeaking on again almost gives me a heart attack.

'Attention, Crater Lake.' A familiar voice echoes through the rooms. 'This is Miss Hoche. Please listen carefully to this important information. Some people in the centre, including a handful of

Montmorency pupils, are suffering the negative effects of inhaling paint fumes. These people may appear to be out of sorts. They could be displaying some discolouration to the eyes. Do not be alarmed – they are all making their way to the medical centre. It has come to my attention that there are children not suffering from these symptoms out of bed. This is unacceptable. Please return to your rooms and try to get some sleep. Everything will look different in the morning. Hoche out.'

The speakers click off.

Every 'symptom-free' kid steps into the main dorm corridor, as another bunch of bug-eyes (people formerly known as Khalil, Chips, Dennis, Dylan and Emily-Rose) do the whole 'out-of-sorts' walk towards the 'medical centre'. The kids who haven't seen this before are horrified. To the rest of us, it's become like ketchup on a burger. Standard. Adrianne and Big Mak run past them on their way back to join us and barely give them a glance.

'We heard Miss Hoche on the tannoy system,' Adrianne says between gasps for breath. Adrianne is fit, so she must have been running either really fast or really far to be in this shape. 'You can hear it for a long way out of the building.'

'What do you mean out of the building?' I say.

'Surely the medical room is inside.' Chets frowns.

'The medical room *is* inside,' Adrianne says. 'I've seen it on the centre map. Mr Tomkins didn't go to the medical room, and neither did the others. They went out of the building, across the lawn and started climbing up the river side of the crater. We were deciding whether to carry on after them...'

'...But Hoche's speech came out of the air like the voice of doom and we stopped for a second to listen,' says Mak. 'The bug-eyes disappeared into the trees, didn't even flinch. We thought we'd better come back to regroup.'

'So Hoche was lying?' Chets says. 'That doesn't seem right.'

'Of course she was lying – none of what she said makes any sense at all. Why would some people be affected by paint fumes, and not others? And more importantly, since when did paint fumes turn people into bug-eyed zombies with a compulsion to work rather than eat brains?'

'So what's happened to them, then?' Katja says.

'We know we were locked in, right? Maybe Digger pumped some kind of bio-weapon gas in through the vents to our rooms,' Mak says.

'Even if that were true,' Adrianne has already recovered her composure, while Mak is still bent over trying to catch his breath, 'why did it only affect half the class? We're all fine, right?' She looks around to shrugs and nods. 'What was different about the others – the ones who bugged out?'

'They were asleep,' I say.

'Damn, you're right,' says Mak.

'And Miss Hoche said that thing about how we should all try to get some sleep and everything would look different in the morning.' Katja's eyes are wide, and turquoise like a tropical ocean. She looks afraid.

'Everything probably does look different if you suddenly have eyes like a wasp.' Adrianne was right, that's what they looked like – the wasp eyes from the documentary.

'But Miss Hoche wouldn't want to hurt us, would she?' Chets asks the question everyone else is thinking. Everyone except me, that is. I've seen that side of her – the nasty, bullying side. The side that enjoys the power she has over people.

'She was locked in her room and magically got out. She didn't go the way the bug-eyes went, or we would have seen her. She apparently has control of the tannoy' (yeah, I say it like I always knew what it was called – thanks, Adrianne) 'system and is using it to tell us what to do. If she was worried about the others like we are, she would have come and spoken to us about it face-to-face.'

'She does love to get in our faces,' Mak says.

'I don't know what the hell is going on, but I think we have to assume that she's involved somehow.' They all look at me and I can see how confused they all are – confused and scared. The funny thing is, I'm not. There's a puzzle that needs solving, and people who need assurance and protection. And I'm tingly excited cos I know I'm the best person to get us all through it. To me, it feels like the start of an adventure.

'So we're not going back to our rooms to get some sleep, then?' Chets says.

'No, we're definitely not doing that.'

'Then what *are* we going to do?' Katja says.

'First, we'll quickly go back to our rooms,' I say.

'Are you completely dense, Fangs? We have to go somewhere and hide.' Trent has been quiet for a bit but I think he senses that people are listening to me, and he really hates it.

I turn and start running down the corridor, back to my little cubby-hole bedroom.

'What are you doing?' Adrianne calls.

'We have a bit of time while they think we're going back to bed,' I shout back. 'We need to get everything out of our rooms that we can use.'

'Like what?' Chets shouts. 'What can we use?'

'Food, water, anything we can carry. And, most importantly, this is not the type of situation in which we want to be wearing pyjamas,' I say. 'If we're preparing for some kind of battle, we need to put some clothes on.'

'Good idea,' says Adrianne. 'We'll all get changed and meet back at Lance's room in five minutes.'

Fourteen of us gather outside my room: me, Chets, Big Mak, Katja, Adrianne, Trent, Trent's friends – Noah, Krish, Luca, Jayden and Rav – and three other girls from Katja's dorm – Celine, Prit and

Gracie. There aren't as many of us as I'd hoped, but I'm thinking we're lucky that any of us survived the lock-in. If it wasn't for me being in that out-of-the-way, 'special' basement room, I would have been locked in, too. I can only think that whoever locked us in – and I'm thinking Digger, Hoche or some as-yet-unseen baddy (cos let's face it, there always is one) – must have forgotten about my door.

We're dressed and ready to go, with full pockets and backpacks.

'I feel like I should be wearing heavy-duty combat gear,' I say. 'Maybe with a bullet-proof vest and a really large weapon.'

'And some kind of helmet,' says Katja.

'In this weather, you'd dehydrate and die in hours,' says Mak. 'What you need is versatile, lightweight coverage, preferably something in a camouflage print.'

'Or layers,' says Adrianne. 'I have my cag-in-a-bag in my backpack. You never know when you might need a waterproof.'

'Maybe I should go back and get my hoody,' Chets says. 'I don't want to get cold.'

'Chets, buddy, there's not going to be a sudden blizzard.' I'm aware that time is passing quickly, we don't know where Hoche or Digger are, and we're losing focus. 'We're moving now. Whatever we've got, we've got. Anything else we need we'll have to find as we go.'

'Go where exactly?' Trent says.

'We need to gather information and stay undetected. To do that, we need to keep moving around the centre.'

'Why do we need information? Kids have turned into wasp-faces, our teacher is trying to make us turn, too. What more do we need to know? We find a central place where we can all hang out and wait for help to arrive.'

'You mean we should hide?' I say.

'I'm good with hiding,' says Chets, tugging on my sleeve like a toddler.

'If we all hide in one place, they're going to find us. Quickly,' I say.

'So we barricade ourselves in. We could use the dining hall – move those big tables across the doors. The windows are high, so they won't be able to climb in through those. You see, I've thought of everything. That's why I'm head boy.'

'No, no, no.' I shake my head. 'This is a bad plan. And not just because it's yours.'

'What's the problem, Fangs? I thought you loved trapping people in places.'

'That's exactly it, Trent. If you barricade yourselves in, you're trapped. Haven't you seen this exact scenario in a million films and books and on the TV? When people barricade themselves in, it never works. The barricades don't hold, or the bad guys find some other way in – the roof, the air vents, underground tunnels. There is always a way.'

'You're just scared we're going to see you in your true form, when your fangs grow extra-long and wings sprout out of your back.'

'You're right. That's exactly why I'm saying we shouldn't go through with your stupid plan.'

I turn to the others. 'Listen. I've played a lot of strategy games. The key to survival in these situations is to keep moving. We need to know what we're dealing with. We'll probably need to collect supplies as we go. We need to stay one step ahead of the enemy. We shut ourselves in a room and we might never get out. Or at least the real usses won't get out.'

'Why should we trust you? All you do is play computer games, like those YouTube losers. You can't even kick a football. I'm head boy, so I get to decide,' Trent says.

Actually, I can kick a football, just not very well.

'I don't see how the ability to kick a football is even relevant here,' I say. 'Plus, this is a life or death situation, so normal leadership hierarchies don't apply. It's every man for himself, and I'm not going to follow someone who's going to get me bugged.' There is no way I'm doing what Trent wants. I'm hoping that everyone else will see how suicidal his plan is.

'I'll Geek, Robot, Overlord you for it,' he says.

'Fine,' I sigh. 'One, two, three…'

'Overlord!' Trent says, doing the Overlord action, which is thumping down both fists on the arms of your throne. At the exact same time, I say 'Robot!' and robot smash his fists aside. I told you, he always plays Overlord.

'Best of three,' he says.

'No one called best of three,' Big Mak says. 'Lance won and you'd better deal with it, son.'

'Go slither around the centre, then. We don't want you anyway. You'd be a liability.' Trent is such a good loser.

'Fine. You guys can do what you want. I'm going.'

'Lance, you can't!' Chets looks terrified.

'Chets, I know it seems easier to sit tight and hope someone comes to help us, but sometimes the easiest choice isn't the right choice. I don't want to turn into one of those whatever-they-ares, so I'm going. You should come with me.'

'Are you sure, though?' Chets looks at me. 'Are you sure this is the right decision?'

'I'm as sure as I can be given that I've never been in a situation like this before. I've never let you down, have I?'

'No.'

'Or allowed you to get hurt?'

'No.'

'Then maybe you should trust me.'

'I'm with Lance,' Big Mak says. 'Holing up is only a good idea when all other options have been exhausted. And holing up with Trent sounds worse than being chased by killer activity-centre workers.'

'I'm coming, too,' says Katja. 'I trust Lance. Maybe we can find a way out of here without waiting two more days for the coach to come back.'

'OK, so Big Mak, Katja, Chets…?'

Chets nods.

'And me are going. If anyone else wants to come, you can.'

The rest of the class stay standing behind Trent, looking afraid, as they totally should because they're about to get attacked-slash-murdered by a bunch of psychopaths in matching polo shirts, or turned into human-wasp hybrids.

'Your funeral,' I say. Having the safety of my friends on my head is a massive deal, and I don't know why I'm so sure that I'm doing the right thing. I just feel it.

We turn and start to walk away.

'Wait!' a voice calls out. 'I'm coming with you.' Adrianne runs to join us.

'I thought you and Trent were, you know, besties,' I say.

'Trent is a jumped-up imbecile,' she says. 'I hope he barricades himself into the dining hall so effectively that he can't get out and I never ever have to see his annoying, smug face again.'

'Not besties, then,' I say.

Katja giggles. She has a sweet giggle – it sounds like jingly bells.

'Just because he's head boy and I'm head girl, it doesn't mean we're anything alike, and it definitely doesn't mean I have a thing for him.'

'Hey, I never said anything about a thing.' I put my hands up as if I'm dealing with a raging lion, which I kind of am because Adrianne is scary.

'Like I said, THERE IS NO THING!' She stomps off ahead.

'Totally glad Ade decided to come with us,' Big Mak says.

'Are you sure she's not one of them?' Chets whispers, obviously afraid of antagonising the beast.

'I'm not one of them, Chetan,' she calls back. 'I'm just sick of people making assumptions about me.'

6
In the Dark, Dark Woods

So we've gone rogue from the rest of the class and I'm happy cos we can be more stealthy as a small group, but I know it also makes us vulnerable.

'Where are we going?' Katja says, as we jog through the centre, away from the dorms.

'We need to find out more about what's going on,' I say. 'So we're going to where the happenings are happening.'

'Into the trees!' Mak whoops.

'But that's where the creepy eyes are,' Chets says. 'Shouldn't we be going the opposite way from there? Plus, it's really late. Maybe we should rest awhile first.'

'We can't rest until we know what we're dealing with. It might not be safe.' I ignore Chets' sad sniff. 'We move quickly and quietly. Keep a lookout for security cameras. As soon as they realise we've gone, they'll start looking for us. There are definitely cameras in the communal areas.'

'And at the entrance,' Adrianne says. 'I think there's one on every corridor.'

'What about outside?' I say.

'I don't think so, but we should probably check.' Adrianne slows down for a second to adjust the straps of her backpack. It looks stuffed full and really heavy.

'Do you want me to carry that for you?' Mak says, jogging alongside her.

'You think because I'm a girl I can't carry my own backpack?'

'Just trying to help,' he says.

'If you want to help, show me a little respect and don't treat me like a princess.'

Mak looks a bit hurt.

'You can treat me like a princess if you like, Big Mak,' Katja says. 'I'm happy for you to carry my bag.'

Mak just huffs and runs on.

'Figures,' Katja says.

I feel like there's some weird vibe and a whole thing going on that I don't get, but now is really not the time to start examining the dynamics between my friends. We reach the side exit, push it open and slip out into the night.

We line up against the wall, hidden in shadow, but knowing we'll have to get across the lawn and obstacle course, and they're lit up like your teeth at the dentists.

'We either go straight across, or the long way around,' Adrianne says. 'Straight over will take two minutes. The long way at least thirty.'

'So we have to go through. Fast and in silence, on the count of three. One, two...'

'Wait!' says Chets. 'I have a stone in my shoe.'

We watch while Chets fiddles with his laces and slowly, slowly takes his shoe off, tips it upside down (I don't see a stone fall out) and puts it back on again. Anyone would think he was stalling.

''K. One, two...'

I'm bracing myself to run, but the bang of a door shutting thuds through the darkness and we all jump back against the wall, squishing ourselves into the deepest part of the dark.

I hear a couple of click-clacks – a sound I'm very familiar with. I see Hoche walking across a small stretch of path and on to the lawn.

'She *is* still wearing her heels,' Katja says.

She isn't walking like the bug-eyes walked. There's no uniformity, no sense of her being spaced out. She's walking in the way she usually walks, like she's busy and important and everyone should get out of her way.

'Can you see her eyes?' Adrianne whispers.

'She's too far away.'

'A second later and she would have caught us running across the grass,' Mak says. 'We'd have been put on reds for the rest of our lives and lost all of our house points.'

'Lucky I had that stone in my shoe,' Chets says.

I have to smile.

Hoche disappears into the trees by the river.

'Is that the way the others went?' I say.

'Yep,' says Adrianne.

'Then let's go.'

We leg it across the lawn to the kind of safety of the trees. There is no wind, and no sign of any birds or animals. The only noise is the clinking of the zips on our backpacks. I've never known quiet like it.

The moon is bright, and when we reach the woods, we find a person-made path through the undergrowth. It's clear that many pairs of shoes have walked this way. Well, not pairs of shoes on their own, cos that would be even more insane.

'Slow and steady now,' I say. 'And I suggest we avoid the path. Let's try to flank them instead.'

'I know you're stressed, but you shouldn't swear,' Chets says.

'He means come at them from the side.' Mak rolls his eyes.

'Still no need for the bad language.'

We move deeper into the trees and work our way uphill, going back to the path only when we have to use the bridge to cross the river. Being on the path leaves us feeling exposed, but the further into the trees we go, the less the moonlight penetrates, so we stumble about, trying not to fall in the darkness. After a hundred metres or so, I hear distant noises. Not talking, though – banging and scraping.

'What the hell is that?' Mak whispers. 'I wish I'd brought my night-vision goggles.'

'You have night-vision goggles? Cool,' I say.

'Not so cool when you don't have them on you.'

We edge towards the sound. I expect there to be voices and light, but when we reach the source it's so unexpected that we almost wander right into the middle of it.

I'm up front, so I swing my arm out to stop the others from moving any further forward.

'What the heck?' I say.

We're standing at the edge of a clearing, next to the river, near the top of the crater. The moonlight allows us a hazy view of what's going on. There are no floodlights or lanterns, but small beams of unnatural light shine across the area, coming from various bits of kit around the clearing. Far away to our left there is what looks like a generator, humming loudly and lit up by green lights. Other light comes from tools – chainsaws and a small crane. When I say small, I mean it's not skyscraper high – it's not even as tall as the trees surrounding us, but it's still big enough to lift a medium-sized tree trunk. I know this because that's exactly what it's doing – lifting a medium-sized tree trunk.

Oh yeah, and the whole area is swarming with people. Because the only light is green and red, everyone looks strange and wrong. It's like a freaking zombie disco.

'Can you see the others?' Katja asks.

'It's hard to make anyone out,' I whisper back. 'But at least we know what those bug-eyes are good for.'

'I see Atul and Dennis and Krish,' Adrianne

says. Because apparently, on top of all her other perfections, she can also basically see in the dark.

'There's Mr Tomkins – I see his man bun bobbing about under the crane,' says Katja.

'I think they're all there,' I say, 'but there are loads of adults – deffo more than just Mr Tomkins and Miss Rani.'

'It's all the Crater Lake people,' Chets says. 'You can see their white polo shirts. They're nice actually – I wonder if we can get one at the gift shop.'

'I don't think the gift shop's open, mate,' says Mak. 'They look pretty busy here.'

'It's a hive of activity,' I say. 'But what are they doing?'

We watch for a minute or two. The bug-eyes are working hard and in silence – cutting down trees and moving logs. Some of them are wading in the river, which is wide and deep. They're wearing what look like wetsuits, which seems a bit excessive cos they're hardly in the Arctic Ocean. The water comes up to their chests. Then I see a black mass extending into the water from the far bank.

'What is that?' I ask, squinting at the dark

structure, though I don't know why, cos squinting isn't helping me see it any better.

'They're building a dam,' says Mak.

'Why would they be building a dam?'

'To hold back the water, of course,' says Adrianne.

'Well, that all makes sense, then,' I say.

'I'm confused,' Chets says.

'I think we all are.' Katja rubs Chets' arm.

'So many questions.' I back up slightly and drop into a crouch. The others do the same.

'What are we thinking?' Big Mak says, pulling what looks like a handful of berries out of his pocket.

'Where did you get those?' Chets asks.

'Foraged them on the trail,' Mak says, throwing a few in his mouth in the most chilled-out way possible.

'What if they're poisonous?' I hate to sound like a reception kid, but we all know how dangerous it is to pick wild berries. It's up there with flying a kite near electricity pylons and taking sweets from strangers.

'They're not. They're fine. You want some?'

'Err, no thanks,' I say. 'I think I've got some jelly beans in my bag.'

'Bad idea,' Mak says. 'They're full of refined sugar. You'll get a peak of energy and then crash. You need to get yourself some slow-release carbs.'

'Alright, Bear Grylls.' I have no idea how Mak knows all this stuff, but now's not the time to ask.

'What do we do now?' Katja says. 'We have more information but it feels like we know less than we did before.'

'Hoche,' I say. 'Where did she go?' I turn to Adrianne. 'Can you see her, owl eyes?'

'Give me a minute to scout around,' she says and disappears into the bushes like a black mamba.

I catch Big Mak looking at her like she's his hero.

She's back really fast and beckoning us to follow her. She leads us into the trees a little, and then round to the highest part of the clearing, next to the river. We move towards the bug-eyes again, but this time on our bellies, crawling like commandos, except it's not that cool because my elbows are getting scraped and every part of me is itchy. We go slowly and flinch at every snapping twig. At last, Adrianne stops and points.

About ten metres away, I see Hoche and

Digger. They're leaning against what looks like a heater, like they're trying to warm themselves up. They're talking loudly – the only voices amongst all those people. We stay as still and quiet as we can, and listen.

'There are thirty-four workers now,' Digger tells her. 'We're making good progress, but we're going to need additional hands for stage two.'

Hoche rubs her hands together – I think to warm them, but it could be that classic villain hand-rubbing like you see in the movies. 'We'll have help soon. There are fourteen children asleep in the centre. Once the sporelings awaken we should have thirteen new workers, and a third hunter to help us snare more hosts.'

'And when we free the other spores, the hive will grow exponentially.' Digger smiles, which looks all wrong on his big potato face.

'It's vital that we keep on track. Time is limited. There can be no delays,' Hoche says.

'All potential threats have been dealt with. The centre is in our hands and there is nobody left to stop us. I don't foresee any obstacles.'

'And yet the humans can be so unpredictable. We must stay alert and leave nothing to chance.

We've waited decades for this opportunity – it might never come again.'

The rest of their conversation is drowned out by the sound of a chainsaw cutting through another trunk.

'Poor tree,' says Katja.

I signal to the others that we should retreat. We need to talk. We slide back into the woods and then trek down the crater. I look for some cover, so that we can rest without being seen. On the other side of the lake is a wooden pier and boat shed.

The area is deserted and, if a bug-eye were to come, we could escape across the lake. 'Everyone can swim, right?' I say. They nod and follow. I open the unlocked door to the boat shed and find it empty. It's cooler here by the lake and there's plenty of space for us inside. So finally we stop. I place myself by the door so I'll be able to see anyone coming our way.

'What the hell was that?' Mak says.

'It sounded like Miss Hoche and Digger planning to turn us all into bug-eyed workers while we sleep,' says Katja.

'So that we can build a dam,' Chets says.

'Which is somehow going to free other spores.'

Adrianne unzips her backpack and takes out a bottle of water. 'And, as Miss Hoche referred to all the bug-eyes as sporelings, I expect the spores are what made them...'

'...Bug out,' I say. 'But how will building a dam free the spores?'

Everyone shrugs.

'So, things we know: Hoche is bad; Digger is bad; spores are bad.'

'Ooh – the bug-eyes building the dam – they called them workers,' says Katja, 'And the other type of sporelings they mentioned were called hunters.'

'Like Digger and Miss Hoche,' Chets says.

'And like the wasps,' Adrianne says. 'In the documentary, there were two types of wasps, the ones who work and build the nest...'

'And the ones who look for prey and attack them with their venom.' I swallow a swig of water. 'And there were the parasitic ones, remember? The ones that use their prey's body to hatch their babies in?'

'The caterpillar,' says Chets.

Even in the darkness, I can tell that everyone is making an 'ew' face.

'I hate to focus on the bad bits,' I say. 'But Hoche referred to us as humans.'

'Which implies that she isn't human and nor is Digger,' says Adrianne.

We take a moment. I think all of us are trying to get our heads around the impossible situation we've found ourselves in.

'So, the question is: if they're not human, then what the hell are they?'

7
Spider Monkey

My phone tells me it's almost midnight. I have no reception, no wifi and no 4G, so it's pretty useless for any kind of communication but it's handy as a torch, and I like the reassuring feel of it in my pocket.

Just in case, I text my mum, asking her to send help. I know it's not going to get through, but it would be stupid not to, right?

'What's our next move?' Mak says.

I've been thinking about this. 'We have to warn the others.'

'Why?' Mak says. 'They chose to snuggle up in the dining hall and hope for the best. They could have come with us. They didn't.'

'But still,' I say, 'we have to try – it's the right thing to do.'

'You know Trent would never do this for you, don't you?' says Adrianne.

'I know,' I say. 'But, for once, Trent isn't the enemy. We're under attack from a non-human, aka alien, force. We have to stick together and, above all else, we must remember what makes us human.' I say this partly cos it's in all the alien invasion movies, but also because I've always felt compelled to try to keep people safe. It's my thing. 'Besides, it's in every zombie apocalypse story ever – if you act like a jerk and wimp out of helping others, you always come to an especially bad end. Usually with screaming and lots of blood. Maybe some guts splattered across a wall.'

'So we go to the dining hall and knock?' Katja asks.

'It's worth a try.' I zip up my backpack and sling it over my shoulders.

'They might have food in there,' Chets says. 'I can get some supplies. For all of us, I mean.'

'Let's get this over with before Hoche and Digger realise we're on to them.' Mak pulls on a baseball cap.

Adrianne leads the way out of the boat shed and back around the lake towards the centre. We sprint past the main entrance, back round to the fire exit that we used to get out.

'Don't these doors only open from the inside?' Katja says.

'Yes,' I say. 'Which is why I used a fire extinguisher to prop it open when we left.'

'Are you sure this is your first alien invasion?' Big Mak asks. 'You're like a pro.'

'Strategy,' Chets says, 'is one of Lance's best skills.'

'Well,' I shrug, 'that and my famous film and TV character impressions.'

'You could have your own TV show,' says Katja.

'Will you all, please, focus?' Adrianne says. 'We need to be quiet. We don't know if Miss Hoche and Digger are back in the building. We need to stay alert.'

We tiptoe through the empty corridors. They have those lights that automatically flick on when you get close, so we can see, but it feels like we're going to be discovered at any moment. When we reach the dining hall, Chets knocks on the door.

'I know we're trying to be stealthy, Chets, but they actually need to hear the knock. Invisible sound isn't going to cut it.'

He knocks again, much louder. We wait.

'Screw this,' Mak says, and pushes the door. It doesn't budge. He grabs the handles with both hands and pushes and pulls as hard as he can. 'Guys?' he calls. 'Are you alive in there? We need to speak to you.' There is a rattling on the other side as he shakes the doors, but no answer. 'Oh well, we tried,' he says.

'We need to know if they're OK,' says Katja. 'Is there another way in?'

'Only those windows,' says Chets. 'But they're super high up.'

'Let's go round the other side and check them out.'

We sneak out of the building again, and follow it round to the back of the dining hall. I look up at the windows. They are really high. If you stood four large elephants on top of each other (though I don't know if that's possible cos, although elephants always stand on balls in cartoons, so I know they're good at balancing, I don't know if the bottom one could take the weight of the other three) the top elephant would probably be able to peep into one of the dining-hall windows.

'No way any of us are going to be able to climb up there,' Mak says.

'I think I can,' Katja says quietly, almost like

she's ashamed of it, which is ridiculous, cos anyone who could climb even half that high would legit be a savage.

'Are you sure, Katja?' Chets looks at the wall and then back at Katja.

'If she says she can, then she can,' Adrianne says. 'I don't know why you would doubt her. Is it because she's a...?'

'Human person and not Spiderman?' I say. 'Yes, it is.'

'I'll give it a try,' Katja says. 'Don't all stare at me, though. You'll put me off.'

'We won't stare,' Chets says, and then we all stare as she grabs hold of a pipe and starts climbing up the wall like a flipping monkey.

'My mistake,' I say. 'She is Spiderman.'

Katja makes it to the window. The light from inside illuminates her face, making her look like a golden, wall-climbing angel. She has her elbow hooked around the pipe and her toes balancing on a piece of metal screwed into the wall. It's only about twenty-centimetres long, and not the one thing I'd like standing between me and certain death, but she seems pretty chill about it. She uses her other hand to push at the window. It doesn't budge. She raps on it, as hard as she can without losing her balance, then grabs on to the pipe again and clambers down. When she reaches the ground I hear everyone make a 'phew' sound with their mouths.

'They're in there,' she says, slightly out of breath. 'They're playing cards and chatting in groups. And listening to music, I think.'

'Did they see you, or hear you?' I ask.

'No. They were all mucking around, so I think it was quite noisy.'

'They must have a lookout, though?' I say.

She shakes her head.

'Idiots,' says Mak. Which is basically what we're all thinking.

'Are any of them asleep?' I ask.

'It didn't look like it,' she says. 'Some of them have sleeping bags laid out on the floor, but nobody was lying down.'

'Then it isn't too late for them.' I push my hair back with my hand, trying to think for a moment. 'Look, we don't know how the spores are getting inside people, but we know they turn bug-eyed when they fall asleep. If one of that lot falls asleep in there, all of them could be in danger.'

'But the bug-eyes don't seem that dangerous,' Chets says.

'The worker bugs don't, but the hunter bugs will be,' I say. 'What if one of them wakes up as a hunter?'

'I think we also need to consider that a lot of their behaviour has been wasp-like so far,' says Adrianne. 'And even worker wasps will sting if one of the nest is attacked. They release a pheromone or something, and it puts all the others in defensive mode.'

'Are you saying they're alien-wasp people?' says Chets.

'I'm saying we don't know what they are.' Adrianne has her hands on her hips. 'So we have to consider all options. I don't think we should antagonise any of them.'

'So how can we get a message to the others?' Katja says.

'There's the tannoy system,' says Chets.

'But everyone will hear it. Hoche will know we're on to her.' Big Mak is leaning against the wall, eating what look like bird seeds.

'And she'll know exactly where to find us if we get to the tannoy microphone to give them the message,' I say.

'So we make the message quick, and then run,' Adrianne says. 'Hide somewhere.'

'We need a place they won't think of,' says Katja. 'Or somewhere they wouldn't want to go.'

'That's it,' I say. 'The cold – they don't like the cold. They keep everything hot in the building. They had that heater out by the dam. Digger almost fainted when pre-bug Hoche asked for some cold drinks. He made us hot soup for dinner in this heat, for flip's sake!'

'But this whole place is like an oven,' says Katja.

'There must be a fridge,' says Mak. 'They must have a giant fridge to keep the milk and stuff in.'

'And where would the tannoy mic be?' I say.

'It can only be in the admin office,' says Adrianne. 'I saw it on the map, so I can get us there.'

'Awesome,' I say. I love having a plan. 'So, office, then fridge.'

'I'm not sure it's a perfect plan,' says Chets.

'It's far from perfect,' I say. 'But it's all we've got. And we're going to give it a try either way, right?'

'Right,' everyone says. And we slink back into the centre.

8
The New Rules

As we make our way through the building, stopping at every corner to peek into the next corridor, listening at every door before we open it, and finding the whole place abandoned, I feel a sort of calm contentment. The situation is laid out before me – a series of puzzles and problems to solve. We face one obstacle at a time. We either overcome it, or we don't. I don't have to worry about multiplying fractions, or using subordinate clauses. The only thing I have to worry about is getting past the next challenge.

It's so quiet and so still, but I know this is the calm before the poo-storm. As soon as we use the tannoy system, they'll be after us. We'll be hunted.

We reach the admin area and push open the door. There is a main office – a large space with two desks and chairs and shelves full of files. A door on the right leads to a meeting room. A door at the back leads to another, smaller office and we can see inside it cos there's a glass panel.

'There's a phone,' I say.

'Phones are no good, though – there's no reception.' Chets' breath fogs up the glass.

'Not a *phone* phone,' I say. 'One of those ones from the olden days that my nan has. A landline.'

Big Mak wipes the condensation from the glass and looks in. 'Those phones don't need reception – they work from wires.'

'So we could call for help?' Katja says.

Chets grabs the door handle. 'We could call for help!' He yanks it down and pushes on the door, but it doesn't move.

'What is it with this place and locked doors?' I ask, although I'm secretly pleased because part of me doesn't want to ask for help. Part of me wants to fix this by myself, just to see if I can. Just to prove I can.

'OK. Adrianne – look for keys. Mak – see if there's any possibility of breaking it down. Chets – turn on those computers and see if there's any way of logging in without a password. Katja – look for anything else useful. I'll look for the tannoy system.' I'm really hoping it's not behind that locked door, cos I don't think we're going to be able to get in there.

Everyone gets to work. No talk, just rummaging

and mouse clicking and door examining. I glance around the room. I don't know what I'm looking for but I feel like I'll know it when I see it. In one corner, screwed to the wall, is a black box with a bunch of buttons on it. I look at it carefully. I want to make sure I'm going to get this right before I commit myself to pushing a button. Once I do that, all hell is going to break loose.

'Is it complicated?' Katja comes over and stands with me.

'Well, there's a button that says "push and hold to talk", and a speakery-looking part that says "speak clearly into microphone". So I guess not.'

'Who's making the announcement?' she says.

'Ooh, can I do it?' Adrianne gives up her search for keys and joins us at the black box of destiny.

'I want to!' Chets pushes back his wheelie chair.

'Shouldn't you be trying to crack some passwords?' I ask.

'I've tried all the obvious ones – Password, 1234, Crater Lake, I am an evil alien, my eyes are weird, etcetera. Nothing works.'

'And nothing's going to break down that door,' says Mak, joining us. 'Except some explosives or a wrecking ball.'

'Did anyone dibs it earlier?' One of the nicest things about Katja is that she always tries to be fair.

'Nobody dibsed it. Shall we Geek, Robot, Overlord for it?' Chets says.

'Honestly, guys, it's only a tannoy system,' says Adrianne. 'I don't know why you're all so desperate to use it. Besides – I'm head girl, so it really should be me.'

'Right, let's get a quick drink of water and think this through.' I go over to a water cooler by the window. It's set to 'ambient temperature' whatever the hell that means. I pour myself a cup and knock it back. 'Apparently, ambient means unpleasantly warm,' I say, thinking longingly of the fridge. 'Let's write down what we're going to say, plan our route to the kitchen and take it from there.'

A few minutes later and we're ready to go. We stand around the black box, and on my nod, Big Mak pushes the button.

'Attention, pupils of Montmorency School,' he says. 'This is Maksym talking to you live from Crater Lake.'

'For everyone hiding from Digger and Miss

Hoche – it's really important that you listen to the following message.' Katja takes her finger off the button, then quickly puts it back – 'Love Katja.'

'Many classmates scraped their knees and risked their lives to bring you this information.' I say. 'We have learnt that Digger and Hoche have become part of some alien race and their job is to hunt us down and turn us into the bug-eyes you saw earlier.'

'They're planning something – the extent of which we don't yet know.' Adrianne's ponytail swings as she talks. 'But we will make it our mission to find out. In the meantime, you must follow these new Crater Lake rules.'

'Don't go anywhere with a member of staff,' says Chets. 'They are all your enemies.'

'Don't follow any instructions they give you. I repeat, do not do as you're told. Mak out.'

'And, most importantly,' says Adrianne. 'Do not fall asleep. If one of the group falls asleep, evacuate them from your secure area. Don't try to keep them with you or they will attack you. Just let them go – they're already lost.'

'We know people only turn when they're sleeping but we don't know exactly how,' I say. 'So keep each other awake, and hang tight – we're working on a plan to get us out of here.'

'Good luck, everyone,' Katja says.

'And remember…' I hold down the button as we all shout into the mic, '…DON'T FALL ASLEEP!'

We're at the office door before the speakers stop reverberating, running down the corridor as fast as we can.

9
Dale's Stash

The kitchen is at the centre of the building, but down a flight of stairs like my room was, as though it's in the basement.

I hold the door while everyone piles in and take one last look behind us before I pull it quietly closed.

'Food!' says Chets, gleefully grabbing a baguette and some apples from a counter.

'Weapons!' Mak whoops, grabbing a rolling pin, a frying pan and a potato masher.

The rest of us do a perimeter of the room to find the fridge. At the very back, down another set of steps, is a huge metal door.

'This must be it,' I say. 'I hope it's not full of dead bodies.' Then, 'Joke!' when I see Katja and Adrianne's horrified faces. 'It would be a waste of good alien hosts to kill people.' I pull the handle and heave the door open. The cold instantly blasts me in the face. It feels so good that I don't even care about the horrid smell of cold meat.

Inside is a small room lined with shelves holding giant tubs of butter. Well, not butter but that cheap stuff that's supposed to taste the same as butter but blatantly doesn't. There are rows of two-litre bottles of milk, stacks of ham, piles of cucumbers and salad stuff – basically a tonne of food. And it's awesomely, refreshingly cold.

'Everybody in!' I check the door to make sure it opens from the inside as well as the outside while they all rush into the room.

'This is fabulous!' Adrianne presses her face to a shelf.

Katja lies on the floor, stretching out across the fridge so that her fingertips touch one side and her toes the other. Chets sinks to his knees and tears into the baguette, alternating a mouthful of bread with a mouthful of apple. Then he opens a crate of butter and starts scooping it out with his fingers. You'd think he hadn't eaten for a week. I open a bottle of milk and tip my head, taking a huge mouthful which I quickly spit all over Mak.

'Gone off?' He laughs.

'Just a bit,' I say. 'I guess they've not been keeping their refrigerated supplies in order.'

'That's a good sign. Hopefully they won't come

in here.' Adrianne's cheeks are pink in her pale face. The light in here is bright and stark, so every detail is illuminated: the short fuzz of Big Mak's blond hair; a graze on Chets' arm that surprisingly I haven't heard him complain about even once; the sparkle in Katja's eyes. And a little nest of random belongings tucked behind jars of mayonnaise under the deepest shelf in the corner of the room.

'What's that?' I say, walking over and moving the mayo out of the way. 'It looks like we weren't the only people to think this would be a good hiding place.'

There's a stack of papers, an iPad and a dark red hoody balled up at the back.

'I knew I'd need my hoody.' Chets grabs it and shakes it out. A wallet falls out of the pocket.

Katja picks it up and opens it, pulling out the credit cards and a driver's licence. 'Oh gosh,' she says. 'Look – it's Dale.'

We stare at the card she holds up. It's a National Union of Students, University of Nottingham ID card. Dale is smiling out at us – the same guy we saw earlier, just less bloody and mental.

'Do you really think we're safe here?' Chets says. 'Things didn't go so well for Dale.'

'We're not safe anywhere,' I say. 'But maybe we can find something amongst this lot that will help us.'

'I wonder what happened to him,' Katja says. 'I hope he's all tucked up safe in hospital, eating ice cream.'

'Everybody take a couple of pages and read,' I say. 'We don't know how much time we have here.'

Adrianne, Katja, Mak and I grab some sheets from the pile. Some of them are ripped out of textbooks, some of them have diagrams drawn all over, but most of them are handwritten notes. Scribbles and things scrubbed out with strange comments written at funny angles. The room goes quiet except for the hum of the fridge and the sound of Chets crunching through his apple.

'There's a load of stuff about extra-terrestrial matter,' says Katja. 'That means things that aren't from Earth, right? But what things exactly?'

'Maybe the spores?' I say.

'But how would they have got here if they're extra-terrestrial?'

'Oh – remember in the leaflet it said that the crater we're in, where the lake formed and the centre was built, was created when a meteor hit the Earth?' Of course Adrianne was paying attention when Hoche was reading us the information.

'A meteor from space,' Chets says.

'So what if the spores Hoche mentioned were inside the meteor and were left behind in the crater when the meteor was cleared away?' I'm getting excited as each piece of information fits with the next.

'Alien spores.' Mak looks around at us with a look on his face like this is the coolest thing ever.

I skim through the rest of the notebook page. 'It says here that the spores are tiny – so small they can only be seen through a microscope. He must have managed to get a look at one cos he's drawn a pic.'

Everyone squints at the diagram I'm holding. It looks like a cross between a dandelion seed and an angry giant squid.

'And this page says that they thrive in super-hot conditions,' says Katja.

'They're called extremophiles,' Mak says. 'My parents make me watch loads of documentaries so I know about this stuff.'

That seems a bit weird: Mak's parents aren't

even bothered whether he does his homework or not, but I guess they must value a different kind of education.

'Do you think that when they started building the centre, the digging and stuff freed the spores?' Chets has finally put down his lunch-slash-breakfast-slash-I don't even know what mealtime it is, and picked up some of Dale's papers to look at.

'And there's the heatwave! It hasn't been this hot for a hundred years, or something,' says Mak.

'It hasn't been this hot since records began,' Adrianne corrects him. 'And it hasn't rained in weeks.'

'So they like it hot and dry,' I say. 'Which works with what we've seen so far – them keeping away from anything cold and … flipping heck – the dam! They're trying to stop the river from flowing down into the crater!'

The tannoy system crackles on. 'Montmorency pupils – this is your assistant head speaking. It seems you ignored my instructions to stay in your rooms. That is unacceptable behaviour. Those of you in hiding – I will give you another chance to come to me and surrender. Whatever that rogue group of naughty children have told you, believe me it is in your best interests to do as you are told. And for the rest of you running around the centre causing mischief, let there be no doubt: I am in control of Crater Lake, and I will make you comply with my wishes. You have fifteen minutes to come to the main office and give yourselves up or there will be severe consequences. The clock is ticking.'

'She sounds really mad,' Katja says. 'What if she finds us?'

'I've been thinking about that.' I shove Dale's notes into the pocket of his hoody, ball it up and squash it into my backpack.

'Surely we need to keep looking at those pages?' Adrianne says. 'Why are you putting them away?'

'Because there's something else we need to do first, to try to slow down Hoche and Digger. Do you remember where the security room is, Ade?'

'Of course,' she sniffs. 'It's at the far end of the centre, why?'

'We need to do something about the security cameras. With them all functioning, she can track us too easily. If we can turn them off, she'll be blind.'

Mak pulls his cap back on. 'Good thinking, mate. Let's go.'

'It was getting too cold in here anyway,' Katja says, retying her shoes.

'Ready then?' I say. 'Let's go. As fast as we can.'

10
The Hacker

We leave the gorgeous coolness of the fridge and run through the kitchen, grabbing supplies and bottled water as we go. I listen at the door before inching it open and looking up and down the corridor.

'Back in the fridge! Back in the fridge!' I try to make my voice quiet but commanding at the same time, which is actually quite hard. 'Bug-eyes!' I say, and that gets everyone moving, shoving each other towards the fridge door. We bundle in and I pull it so that it's open just a crack.

'Hunters?' whispers Mak, trying to see over my shoulder.

'No, from the way they were walking, I think just workers. But we can't afford for them to see us. Hopefully they're just passing through.'

But, as I hold my breath and start to count a minute out in my head, I see the handle of the kitchen door turn, and two people enter the room.

'Guys,' I say, 'I know what happened to Dale.'

Dale is still in his dirty, bloody clothes, but his wounds have been neatly bandaged, and the bleeding has stopped. The dark, swollen rings around his eyes have gone.

'Ah, he looks so much better.' Katja is crouching down peeping at him from under my arm. 'Apart from the bug-eyes, obviously.'

'But how did he get here?' Chets says.

'Digger obviously had him brought back here instead of calling an ambulance,' Adrianne says. 'And he was unconscious, remember, so he must have bugged out.'

'Look, he's with Midge,' Mak says. 'Shouldn't they be working, though? At the dam site? What are they doing?'

They've disappeared over to the window side of the kitchen and out of view. I edge out of the fridge and creep to the corner to look.

'We must hurry,' says Midge, in a calm voice. 'We must get back to work.'

'These bodies need sustenance. The hive cannot work without proper nourishment,' Dale replies.

'These bodies are weak,' says Midge, and that is

106

something Midge would never say, because she's a purple belt/white stripe in karate and she bangs on about it all the time. 'They require so many things.'

'They are all we have. They will suffice.' Dale is putting a huge pot on the cooker. I'm satisfied that they don't know we're here and that we just have to sit tight, so I return to the fridge, close the door and signal the others to hide behind the shelves until they're gone.

'What are they doing?' Chets returns to his baguette.

'Making food,' I say.

'What are they having?'

'I'll give you one guess.'

'Tomato soup!' they all whisper at the same time.

'Wrong. Chicken soup.'

As soon as Midge and Dale are gone, we race out of the kitchen. Time is running out. We don't come across any more bug-eyes as we run through the empty corridors. I assume they're all tucking into their soup in the dining hall.

I'm not sure what the worker bug-eyes will do if they catch us. I know they're not hunters, and that their focus is carrying out whatever tasks they've been set, but as they're all reporting to Hoche, we can't risk being seen by them.

The security-room door has a 'No Entry – Staff Only' sign on it, which (lucky for us) somebody must have thought would be enough to stop a bunch of kids from running in and messing with their stuff.

Inside the room there are three screens that flick through images of the centre – the security gate, the entrance to the building, the corridors and some of the rooms.

'There are the others,' Katja says, as the inside of the dining hall appears.

'It looks like they're arguing.' Chets leans in to get a better view. 'Trent seems mad – that's not good.'

'Maybe some of them want to leave,' says Adrianne. 'They've been locked in with him for hours – they're probably desperate to get out.'

'You really don't like him, do you?' I say. 'What's the story?'

'Why does there have to be a story?' she snaps at me. 'You all hate him too.'

'But he spends his life trying to make ours miserable. He's nice to you.'

'I never asked him to be.' Adrianne's face has turned red. 'In fact, I wish he'd stop. Now can we change the subject?'

'Guys,' Mak says, peering at one of the screens. 'Check this out.'

On the screen, in black and white, we can see Digger skulking around in a room we haven't seen yet. It looks like some kind of maintenance area cos there are hoovers and cleaning stuff, and what could be a boiler. As we watch, Digger lifts a heavy-looking lid from a giant container.

'What's in there?' I ask.

'It looks like the water tank,' Mak says.

Digger leans over the open tank, and something flies from his mouth into the water. Because the footage is black and white, and the room is dark, it's really hard to make out, but…

'Did he just spit?' Katja says.

'Oh, man, that's gross.' Chets makes a face and turns away, but the rest of us squeeze in even closer.

'Why would he spit in the water?' I say. 'I mean, I get it could be some kind of revenge spit, but it seems strange for him to go to all that trouble when there are plenty of other things he could do to us.'

The image disappears and is replaced by a view of the admin office. Hoche is in there, pacing around in her heels. Even though there's no sound, I can almost hear the click-clack as she walks back and forth. As she gets to the window side of the office and turns back towards the camera, we see her face clearly. It looks like she's speaking.

'Is she talking to herself?' I say.

'There must be someone in there with her,' Katja says. 'She always tells me that talking to myself is a sign of a disorganised mind.'

'We know it's not Digger.' Chets moves back towards the screen. 'Because he's apparently busy contaminating the water supply. Do you think it's one of the bug-eyes?'

'I think there's a second camera in the office,' I say. 'So when the footage cycles forward, we might be able to see more.'

We wait in silence for a few seconds for the image to change and, when it does, we see there is someone else in the room. There's a figure sitting on a chair. Because of the angle of the camera we can't see his face, but he looks kind of familiar.

'Who is that?' Mak says.

'I'm not sure,' says Adrianne. 'But he can't be a bug-eye – look, he's tied up!'

Adrianne's right. The mystery man is tied to the chair.

'I wish I could hear what she's saying to him,' I say. But even if it is possible to get some sound, we don't have time. 'Can you turn these off, Chets?'

Chets has been inspecting the system. 'Sure, I can turn them off, but what's to stop Hoche turning them back on again?'

'You're right,' I say. 'Can you disable the system, somehow? I'm not talking major hack stuff or implanting a virus: something quick.'

Chets sits at the desk and starts clicking the mouse. 'It's password protected, but if I can crack it…' He taps away at the keyboard.

'Where do we go next?' Katja says. 'It's nearly morning and Miss Hoche is going to be looking for us.'

I look out of the window to see a haze of pale yellow easing up over the horizon. 'I think we'll be safer out of the building. We can find somewhere to hide in the woods while we work out what the hell we're going to do.'

'Cracked it!' Chets yells. One by one, the

images flicker and the screens go dark. 'And I've changed the password to something they'll never guess, so they won't be able to log back in.'

'Awesome. Well done, mate.' I turn to the door but, on second thoughts, I pick up a chair and smash it into the screens, totally destroying them. 'Just in case.'

We leave the room, and make our way to the nearest exit. The sooner we're away from this building, the better.

We trek through the trees as the sun rises, keeping to the steeper side opposite the dam site. As the adrenaline buzz fades away, so does our energy. My backpack feels like it's full of rocks. My legs are starting to refuse to lift my feet. In my head, I offer them bribes – just a bit further and we'll have a sit down; just a bit further and we'll take off our shoes. But, at the same time, I'm worried about stopping cos I feel like I won't want to start again. None of us are chatting now. Our heads are down as we concentrate on each step forward.

'This is a good place,' Mak says, stopping to look around. 'There's a hollow inside those bushes, see, and if we keep a lookout at the top of that tree over there, we'll be able to spot the bug-eyes coming from a long way off. We'll be able to evacuate before they reach us.'

He says it like he knows exactly what he's doing, so I nod and point to a small gap in the bushes.

''K – let's do it. There's enough room in there for everyone, but we'll take it in turns to be lookout. I think we should have two people on duty at all times. I don't want anybody to be alone.'

'Should we have a meeting first?' Adrianne says. 'I think we need to discuss our options.'

Everyone groans.

'Ade is right,' I say. 'We can't just hang around in a bush and hope for the best. Let's eat and talk.'

We sit at the bottom of the lookout tree, except Katja, who climbs up it far enough to give her a good view of the crater.

'Can you still hear us, Katja?' I call, as quietly as it's possible to call to someone who's halfway up a really tall tree.

'Loud and clear.' Her voice floats through the leaves.

Now that we've sat down, the muscles in my legs start to throb and I have an overwhelming urge to lie back and close my eyes.

Looking around at the others, I can see the tiredness is hitting them too. We've been awake for twenty-four hours, which is probably a record for most of them. I've had a lot of sleepless nights, so it's nothing new for me, but even I'm feeling tired. They must be ready to drop.

'What are we going to do, Lance?' Chets leans back against a tree and rubs his eyes.

'We've got through the night,' I say, 'And that's something to be proud of. Does anyone know when the coach is coming back for us?'

'Tomorrow morning,' says Adrianne.

'So we have to get through one day and one night. That's not so bad.' Even as I'm saying it, I know nobody's going to buy it. We're basically done and we have twenty-four hours left before we can get out of here. Even if we can avoid being captured by the hunters, there's no possible way we're going to stay awake. 'We need to understand how the spores infect people, and why it only happens when they're asleep. Maybe we can find some way around the not sleeping thing.'

'Or we need to find a genius way of staying awake,' says Chets.

'When my baby sister was crying all night, my

mum used to take caffeine pills to get her through the days.' Adrianne is putting a plaster on her blister. Only she would have a first-aid kit in her backpack. 'Maybe we'll be able to find some in the centre.'

'OK, caffeine pills,' I say. 'Don't sound like they'd be parentally approved but we can give that a go, if we can find some. What else?'

'Coffee. My mum drinks coffee to wake herself up in the mornings,' says Chets.

'Yes, coffee is definitely an option, even though it tastes like cow poo. Any other ideas?'

Everyone looks defeated.

'We just need to keep busy and help each other out,' I say. 'Let's look at Dale's notes again and see if we can learn anything useful.'

I get out the notes and put the pages in the middle, so everyone can see them. There's no wind in this stupidly hot crater, so they're not going to blow away.

I pick up a scrap of paper with the title 'Intracellular Parasites'. It seems as good a place to start as any.

'Guys,' I say, without looking up from Dale's scribbles. 'I think I've found something. There's a lot of really science-y words that I don't completely understand, but I think what he's basically saying is that the spores are drawn to unconscious brains. If the mind is awake, the spores can't take hold.'

'But how do the spores get to the hosts?' Adrianne asks. 'Did Digger pump them into the centre through the vents? If he did then we might be safe out here.'

I read on for a moment. 'You're not going to like this. The spores are already in the air, too small for us to see. We have to assume that the whole crater is full of them.'

'So they're flying around us right now?' Katja calls down from the tree.

'Yeah, I think so.'

Chets clamps his hand over his mouth and nose and tries not to breathe.

'You're awake, Chets, they're not going to go for you if you're awake.'

'But that means none of us can go to sleep, at all, until we leave the crater,' Mak says.

Everybody visibly shrivels like deflating balloons. Even Katja, though I can't see her, makes the branches rustle in a way that suggests severe shrivelling.

I try not to shrivel myself, cos I feel like it's my job to keep the group's spirits up, but yeah, it's pretty much the worst news ever. Then I look at Chets, who still has his hands over his face like the world's worst gas mask, and I have an idea.

'I've thought of something that might help,' I say. 'But I'm going to have to go back into the centre to get it.'

'Shall we all go?' Adrianne starts zipping up her bag.

'No, it'll be quicker and easier if I go on my own,' I say.

'You said yourself that nobody should be alone,' Katja calls down through the leaves. 'At least take one person with you.'

'Seriously, I've got this. I don't need anyone to come with me.'

'No way,' says Mak. 'It's not happening. Deal with it.'

I'm annoyed cos this is something I really don't want anyone else to be involved in. But I can't argue with my own rules. Chets is yawning his head off and I feel like if I don't get him moving, he's just going to fall asleep. Besides, out of everyone, he's the person I trust the most.

'Come on, Chets – we're going,' I say.

'What?' Chets jumps.

'We're going on a mission back to the centre.'

'But we've only just got here.'

'I know, mate, but this is important – it might mean we can finally get some sleep. And, anyway, you're my best friend and I really need you with me on this one.'

'Just let me have a drink of water,' he says. I knew he wouldn't be able to argue with the best friend card.

In two minutes, we're walking back down the hill, leaving the other three to keep watch and examine Dale's life-saving notes. My legs are screaming at me to stop, but I chew on some gum and do my best to ignore them.

'Chets and Lance on an epic adventure,' I say, to cheer Chets up. The tiredness is bringing out everyone's grumpy side.

'We'll have loads of adventures together at Bing,' Chets says.

I don't know what to say. I know I'm never going to Bing. My grades are average at best. I have a bad attendance record. I have trouble concentrating. Hoche had a black mark against my name long before the whole trapping Trent in the toilet incident. Chets has this blind faith in me cos I saved him from that wasp and basically stopped him from getting picked on through the whole of school. He just doesn't want to see the truth.

'Let's get through this first, and then we'll talk about Bing.'

'Why? Do you think we're going to die? Or get turned into bug-eyes?'

'I'm not saying that. I just feel like we need to focus our efforts on the task ahead of us.' That sounds convincing, right?

'What is it we're going back into that hellhole for anyway?'

'It's a long story,' I say.

'So you won't tell me?'

I can tell I've hurt his feelings. He thinks I tell him everything. Sometimes I get tired of being the responsible adult – he can be such a baby.

'Give me a break, will you?'

He sniffs, and I can just imagine the look in his chocolatey eyes – like a toddler who just had his cuddly bunny taken away. I can't deal with this now. We have to get into the centre and we have to get this done.

We walk in silence, and I'm pretty sure he's feeling as horrible as I am. It's only 8am and the sun is burning my skin. I think my freckles have doubled in number since we got here. Usually when you're in the woods, the air is full of that damp, mouldy leaf smell – the smell of dark green. But the woods right now, they smell the same as everything else – dry, crumbly and dead.

We're getting close to the centre and I can hear something that sounds totally out of place.

'What the hell is that?' I say.

'Pachelbel's Canon,' says Chets.

'Say what now?'

'It's a piece of music. Like classical music. My mum loves it. She finds it very relaxing.'

'Now that makes sense,' I say. 'Hoche is trying to get them to fall asleep. She's probably made them some hot chocolate and is handing out fluffy slippers, too.'

'I want to go home.'

He sounds so sad that I stop being annoyed with him and want to give him a hug. 'Tomorrow, Chets. We'll be going home tomorrow.'

I wonder how that feels – to be homesick. I miss home, but in a different way. I feel guilty that

I'm not there, and guilty that I'm kind of happy to not be there – even with the alien invasion and everything.

It only seems five minutes since we left basecamp – we should call it basecamp, right? – but we're already at the treeline.

We crouch behind some tall ferny stuff.

'Right,' I say. 'I'm thinking they're going to be concentrating on the others in the dining hall. They will have found them by now, and judging by the calming tunes, I'd say they're trying to get them to crack.'

'That's bad.'

'It is for them, but it's good for us. It means we have a better chance of getting in and out undetected.' Then I have a sudden realisation, like a kick in the boy bits. 'How are we gonna get in? None of the doors are proper open and the main entrance is locked.'

Chets does this little smile. It's the first smile I've seen from him since we got here.

'What?' I say.

'When I accessed the security system, I set all the doors to unlock,' he says. 'We can get in any of them without any trouble.'

'Chets.' I punch him (gently) on the arm. 'You're a legend.'

We go for the door that's furthest away from the dining hall. The good thing about the music is that it covers any noises we make. The bad thing is that we won't be able to hear if someone is coming. So we go carefully – stopping to check ahead and behind whenever we reach a door or a junction. Now that we're in danger again, the desperate need to sleep eases a little. Not completely though – I still feel it burning in my eye sockets and tugging at my arms and legs, always dragging me down.

'What's the plan if we run into someone?' Chets whispers.

'Run,' I say. 'Back into the woods if you can, and try to shake them off. If you can't lose them, then the fridge, I guess. You'll be stuck in a dead end but you can block the door and buy some time.'

'I hope whatever we've come to get is worth the trouble,' Chets says.

'Me too.'

'Montmorency pupils.' Hoche's voice oozes through the tannoy speakers like toxic slime. 'I hope you are finding the music soothing. I know you're tired.' Instead of the shrill voice she usually uses for telling us off and shrieking out orders, she's speaking in a lower, gentler tone – it's almost like she's purring. 'You're so very tired and staying awake is too hard. I know your eyelids are drooping. I know your bodies ache to lie down. You don't have to fight it – no harm will come to you if you give in and close your eyes. You'll feel better, stronger, more energised. You'll wake with a clear mind, knowing your place in the world and exactly what you should be doing. The confusion and fear will be gone. So sleep, my lovelies, just sleep.'

Chets puts his fingers in his ears. 'Do you think she can hypnotise us through our ears?'

'And for those of you who choose to fight,' she says, some of that familiar sharpness coming back into her voice, 'know this: your efforts will be futile. The hive is stronger than you. You will fail. We have other ways of making you sleep.' The music comes back on – the same tune over and over again. It's enough to make anyone slip into a coma.

'What other ways, Lance? What's she talking about?'

'I don't know, Chets,' I say. 'But let's hurry, cos I don't want to find out.'

We've reached the sleeping area. Chets keeps lookout at the top of the stairs down to my room, while I go in and grab what I need from where it's hidden under my bed. It's heavy, so it will slow us down on the way back, but I think it's worth the risk. I put it in the empty backpack I brought with me and heave the straps over both shoulders. I can do this.

Chets nods the all-clear, so I jog up the stairs and we make our way back down the corridor. The music seems louder than before – it fills my head and hums through my body and makes our journey towards the exit feel like a sinister dream sequence. I start to zone out and for a moment I wonder if I have actually fallen asleep and that none of this is really happening.

That is until we turn into a corridor and see Hoche standing at the other end.

11
The Chase

She sees us at the exact same moment that we see her and starts walking slowly towards us. The look on her face is somewhere between hate and joy and her eyes – her eyes are glowing. The centres of them are dark like the other bug-eyes we've seen, but the black is ringed with wasp yellow. While the worker bug-eyes looked blank, free of emotion and expression, Hoche's look focused and cruel. Like the eyes of a hunter, I guess.

Other than that, she looks the same: same skirt and jacket, same dangly earrings, same hair that she always puts up in a twist thing, but that always seems like it doesn't want to stay put. It's like her hair is trying to escape from her. And of course, she's wearing her Hoche heels (™).

'Lance and Chetan,' she says. 'How delightful to see you.'

'Can't say the same,' I say, not moving, waiting to see what she'll do next.

'Hi, Miss Hoche.' Chets gives her an uncomfortable smile.

'You two have been giving us quite the run-around.' She takes another step towards us. 'You've been busy.'

'Yep, busy not turning into alien wasp creatures,' I say. 'Unlike you.'

My brain is running through our options. The corridor that leads to the exit is halfway between us and Hoche, to the right. To reach the corridor we'll have to run towards her. I'm assuming we're faster and will get there first, but who knows what becoming an alien does to your running ability. We can either turn back and run to a different exit, which means going much further, or we can risk it. It's a flipping huge decision. Life or death stuff.

'Come with me now and I'll overlook the destruction of property, the disobedience, the rudeness and all your other misdemeanours.' She tips her head to the side. 'I'll even forget the incident that occurred at the start of Year Six.'

It always comes back to this.

'But Lance didn't do that, Miss Hoche,' Chets says, so boldly that I'm taken aback. 'It isn't fair for you to keep blaming him.'

'You don't have to defend me, Chets,' I say, feeling a surge of guilt that's weirdly similar to that hot, vomity sensation you get at the start of a vicious stomach bug.

'Poor, naïve Chetan,' she says, moving her head from side to side like she's warming up for a keep-fit class. 'You really aren't aware of what kind of boy Lance is, are you?'

'I know who he is. He's my best friend and he wouldn't lie to me.'

'Wouldn't he?' she says, looking right at me.

'Ignore her, Chets, she's just trying to get in our heads,' I say, wondering if she's playing for time, waiting for something.

'Tell her once and for all, Lance. Tell her you didn't trap Trent in the toilets.' His trust in me is too much, suddenly, and I'm tired and fed up with having to lie about this over and over again. Especially to Chets.

Hoche smiles, still with the bizarre head and neck movements. 'Don't you think your best friend deserves the truth? You've been holding him back for years. If you're such firm friends, he should know what kind of boy you are.'

'Tell her, Lance,' Chets says.

I'm tired. I'm stressed. I'm trying to decide what to do, which way to run. I'm trying to find a way out. I'm so, so tired.

'I did it, Chets, OK? I shut Trent in the toilets.'

'What?' Chets' face makes my heart hurt. He looks so betrayed. I don't know what to say to him.

There's a half-second break in the music and I hear footsteps behind us. Digger is running down the corridor in our direction. We have Hoche in front and Digger behind. We're out of time. I have to make a choice.

'I don't believe it, Lance,' Chets says.

Time to make a move. We need a head start.

'I shut Trent in the toilets, and I'm glad I did. He deserved it. He knows what he did and, look, here he comes, so you can ask him about it.' I point to the corridor behind Hoche. She takes the bait and turns to look, which gives me a chance to grab Chets' arm and run towards the exit.

She realises she's been tricked a moment later and runs towards us shrieking. But we're going to get to that corridor before she does, I know we are. We have to.

As we reach the turning, I see Digger arrive

where we were standing a few seconds before. They're not going to let us get away. Not without a fight. But we keep running, cos that's the only thing we can do.

'Faster, Chets,' I gasp. I can see the exit.

There's a noise behind us like nothing I've ever heard before – a gurgling, globby sound. I want to look back but I don't want to look back. Then something wet and tinged with yellow flies over my shoulder and splats on the wall.

'What the hell?' I say, and I have to look back.

Hoche and Digger are right on our tails, just metres away. As I watch, Hoche pulls back her head, bubbling and fizzing. Her human mouth opens and two black pincer things grow out of it, stretching her lips outwards until they roll back on themselves. The pincers click together a few times and then widen to allow a blob the size of a tangerine to fly out of her mouth and towards me and Chets. It is the most horrible thing I've ever seen.

'Is Miss Hoche spitting at us?' Chets pants.

'Something like that,' I say.

The spitball hits the floor by my foot and sort of sizzles in a really disturbing way. If I get through this, I know what my nightmares are gonna be about for the rest of my life.

We reach the door and push it open. As it swings shut behind us, I hear another spitball splash into it. We're out of the building, but we're not safe yet. They're right behind us and I don't know how we're going to get away. We can't lead them to the others.

'Where are we going?' Chets asks.

'The lake,' I say. It's our only chance to lose them. I lead Chets across the lawn towards the obstacle course – it'll hold us up, but it should slow the others down, too. We pick our way through the tyres and rope nets as quickly as we can, then storm towards the boat shed.

Then I realise – there's no way I'm going to be able to swim with my heavy bag. It will pull me under in seconds. But I don't want to give it up – we've gone through so much to get it. I scan the area for somewhere to stash it.

There's a roar of anger behind me and I turn to see Hoche's shoe is caught in the rope net. Digger stops to untangle her. This is our chance. There's a gap between the underneath of the pier that goes out into the water and the muddy bank of the lake. I rip the backpack off and shove it into the hole as hard and as fast as I can. It will have to do.

I grab Chets' hand and pull him along the pier to the centre of the lake. 'Jump!' I yell, as Hoche and Digger resume the chase. Chets and me splash into the water. I'd like to say I dive gracefully like an Olympian or a dolphin or something, but diving isn't one of my skills, so it's more like dumping an elephant in the ocean. We splutter to the surface and swim for the opposite shore.

After twenty metres or so, I risk a look back. Hoche is standing on the pier, glaring at us and screaming at Digger, who is in the water, swimming after us. But he's not enjoying it. He's slow and his face tells me he's struggling. I allow myself to breathe – we're going to make it.

We reach the other side of the lake and pull ourselves up out of the water. Every muscle in my body is begging to be allowed to curl up and die, but I force myself on, step by step.

Chets says nothing, just follows me a few paces behind. As we reach the treeline, we turn to see Digger crawling back to the lawn side of the lake, his minotaur butt wiggling from side to side. He and Hoche are having some kind of grown-up discussion, also known as an argument. Whatever it's about, they're going to have a tough time following us. By the time they get around the lake, we'll be long gone and they know it.

We disappear into the trees.

12
Alone in the Crater

'Why didn't you tell me?' These are the first words Chets has spoken since we got out of the lake. After everything we've just been through, I don't think it should matter.

'Jeez, Chets, why are you asking me that now?'

'Because it's important.'

'Our alien teacher just spat venom at us and we barely escaped. We've left the one thing that could help us behind at the lake. Hoche and Digger know we're outside and are going to be hunting us down. Now is not the time.'

Chets stops walking, grabs my shoulder and spins me round to face him. 'But you've had millions of time! It happened nine months ago. Nine months. You could have told me at any point. We spoke about it loads. I defended you when other people accused you! How could you let me do that?'

'It was something I needed to keep to myself. I don't have to justify what I did to you.'

'We're supposed to be best friends. I thought I knew you. How could you do something like that to Trent? How could you lie to me?'

'Like I said to Hoche: Trent deserved everything he got.'

'He didn't deserve to be trapped in the school toilets!' Chets is so angry, I've never seen him like this. 'He missed his entrance test for Bing – if Miss Hoche hadn't persuaded them to let him reschedule, he wouldn't have got in.'

'So what?' I'm so mad with him. Why is he always so stupid and blind to stuff that everyone else can see?

'So that's a jerk thing to do. And then to lie about it. I never thought you were like that.'

'I don't regret anything I've done,' I say, my mind raging, my head thumping. 'Except making friends with you. I should have left the wasp to it. I should have let you get stung.'

Chets chokes out a sob and runs off through the trees.

I stomp off in the opposite direction.

I'm halfway back to basecamp when the realisation of what just happened hits me. And the chasing and spitting seems nothing in comparison to arguing with Chets. All I can see are those chocolate eyes, looking at me like I just decapitated his kitten. Well, maybe not kitten, cos Chets is actually scared of cats. But I've tried to keep him safe from shock and pain for the entire time I've known him. And now I'm the one who's caused it. The anger that burnt through me a few minutes earlier seems to disappear all at once, though it's possible that I sweated a lot of it out, cos I'm dripping wet, and not from my swim in the lake.

Chets is afraid and upset and all alone in the woods. What do I do?

When he ran off it was in the direction of basecamp, so I should go there, find him, apologise. I've been walking fast cos of the rage, but for a while I was going the wrong way. It's easy to get confused in these woods. Trees look like trees. Even when you find one that's especially twisty or covered in ivy and you think, I'll keep that one in my mind so I'll know if I pass it again, five minutes later you've looked at so many other trees that you can't quite picture that twisty ivy tree anymore. You couldn't pick it out of a line-up. But I have developed a strong sense of direction by navigating through various worlds in computer games, so I get back on track.

I'm nearly at the camp and I'm hoping, wishing so hard, that Chets is already there. But when I reach our hollow bush, only Katja, Mak and Adrianne are waiting for me.

'We saw you coming,' Big Mak says. 'Where's Chets?'

'And did you get what you went for?' Adrianne asks.

Katja doesn't say anything. I think she can tell something's gone wrong just from looking at my face.

'I don't know where to start,' I say, bending over, hands resting on my knees, hoping I'm not gonna cry.

'Have some water. And a snack,' Kat says, giving me a bottle from her bag. 'Mak, get back up the lookout tree and we'll have a team meeting underneath.'

I walk to the tree and sit. The swim just about finished my arms and legs, and all I want to do is lay down and sleep. The others aren't looking so good either, and now I have to tell them that not only did I fail, I completely messed things up.

'I got what we needed,' I say. 'But we were caught and chased. Our only chance was the lake, and it was too heavy to swim with, so I left it.'

'And what happened to Chets?' Katja asks. 'Did the bug-eyes get him?'

'No, but Hoche said some stuff – stuff about me and the past and things I've done. As soon as we were safe, me and Chets argued about it and we split up. I thought he'd come back here, but...' I close my eyes for one, two, three breaths. When I open them, Kat and Ade are looking at me, not in a hateful way like I expected, but like I've just rescued their kittens from a house fire and burnt my hands off in the process. Katja and Adrianne are OK with cats.

'So, top priority is to find Chets.' Mak's voice calls down from the tree.

'And then we go back for the bag,' Adrianne says. 'If it's by the lake it'll be much easier to grab than if it was still inside the building.'

'We should all go. Stick together.' Katja starts packing up our things. 'That way we can separate into pairs if we have to. Nobody will be left on their own.'

'And we're going to have to abandon this camp

anyway.' Big Mak is making his way down from the tree. 'Just in case.'

It takes me a second to work out what he means, and then my guts twist when I realise. He means in case they got Chets.

No point in thinking about that now.

I make myself get up as though I'm full of energy and ready for action.

'Oh yeah,' I say. 'There's something else I should tell you, about the bug-eye hunters, I mean.'

'What is it?' Ade says.

'Um … they spit.'

We walk through the woods, calling to Chets as loudly as we dare but there's no sign of him. Every now and then, Mak crouches down to inspect the ground, rub bits of leaf between his fingers or sniff objects he picks out of the mud though I don't even know what they are.

'He didn't come this way,' he says. 'We'll have to try closer to the treeline.

We get quiet as we move nearer to the centre. The hunters know where to look for us now. They could be anywhere: behind that tree; under that bush – well, maybe not that one cos it's prickly, but under a bush; hidden in those shadows. We all look around nervously as we walk, except Mak who is concentrating on tracking Chets.

'He was here,' he says, picking up a bit of broken twig.

'How do you know?' Ade asks.

'Look, you see that patch of ferns.' He points. 'He sat down there, I'd say for at least ten minutes. Then it looks like he got confused about which direction to go in – you can see he was turning around. Look at those marks.'

He points at the ground and I see nothing but dry dirt and some pine needles.

'Then he walked...' He pauses a second and sniffs the air like a flipping Labrador '...this way.' He points back towards Crater Lake.

'He didn't want to stay in the woods on his own,' I say. 'So he went back to the centre to hide.'

This is really bad.

13
The Hunter

'I wish I'd brought my binoculars,' Mak says, trying to see where I'm pointing. 'They're Celestrons.'

'Wow, really?' I say. I have no idea what Celestrons are.

'Yeah, they're as awesome as you'd expect.'

'So you and Adrianne go for the backpack. Me and Kat will look for Chets. We'll meet back at the lake, probably with the hunters on our tails, so be ready.'

'Understood,' Mak says. 'We'll be ready.'

'Be careful, you two.' Adrianne squeezes Katja's hand. 'Look after each other.'

'And you,' I say. And we move towards the building, skirting the treeline. Things have moved on so much since last night – it's like a new level of danger has set in and we're all feeling it. And, you know, being dead tired doesn't help either.

'Where do you want to start looking?' Kat whispers.

'I know Chets as well as I know myself,' I say, 'and there's only one place he's going to be.'

We keep moving right towards the river and I'm sweating cos it's midday and the sun is blazing, and because for the first time since it all kicked off, I'm feeling properly scared. I hate thinking of Chets alone and terrified, and the memory of his look of betrayal plays on repeat through my mind, broken only by images of Hoche with her lips stretched back, pincers out and balls of poison shooting from her mouth.

To get to the gift shop without running straight across the lawn, we have to get close to the dam site, and cross the river over the bridge that the bug-eyes use.

We hear them long before we see them – the movement of lots of people – no chat, just footsteps, the crack of twigs and rustling of trees. We get as close as seems sensible and lie on our bellies in the shrubs to watch.

'Where are they going?' Kat says, as the bug-eyes walk in their steady way, down the path, towards the bridge. Some of them are carrying the tree-cutting equipment. Others are pushing the generator and heater.

'Looks like they've finished the dam,' I say.

'That can't be good.'

'No, it can't. I wonder what the next stage of their plan is.'

'They don't like the water, right?' says Katja, scratching her nose in a really cute way. 'So now they've blocked the river, maybe they're going to try to empty the lake.'

'Once we've got Chets and the backpack, we'll have to try to work out why,' I say.

'But Chets first.'

'Chets first.'

We wait for the bug-eyes to pass and then cross the bridge ourselves. The river isn't flowing fast anymore, but the water hasn't completely gone and I'm sure the bed is sticky with mud. We don't want to leave muddy prints across the centre and give away our movements.

Once we're across, we don't follow the path they took; we keep moving right. This way we'll flank the building and can enter right in the place where I know in my heart Chets is going to be.

The entrance door is unlocked and apparently unguarded. We ease it open and slip into the gift shop.

I see him instantly, standing on the other side of the shop, in front of shelves full of Crater Lake baseball caps, beanies and sunglasses. His back is to us, so I can't see his face, but something about him is different. Maybe it's the way he's standing. Maybe it's because, instead of shaking in a corner, he's out in the open: tall and straight-backed.

'Chets?' I say. 'Are you OK?'

'No thanks to you.' He doesn't turn around.

Something is definitely up. I signal for Katja to stay behind me.

'I'm sorry I didn't tell you about what happened with Trent,' I say. 'But I had my reasons and I hope you know me well enough to believe that they were good.'

'I've been asking myself what I really know about you, and what I've come up with is this...' He turns to face me. He's wearing a Crater Lake polo shirt and sunglasses. There are only two reasons I can think of for him covering his eyes. The first is to hide the fact he's been crying and the second is so awful that I'm going to ignore it and root for reason one.

'We've been so-called friends for five years. In that time you've never invited me to your house.

143

You've only come to mine a few times and only for a couple of hours. You keep secrets from me. You lie to me. You act the big man like you're my saviour or something, but really you just stop me from experiencing anything for myself. You've been controlling me.'

'Chets, that's completely unfair. I've looked out for you and I've done my best to be a good friend. How can you say such horrible things?'

'Because you're nothing special and you've tried and tried to drag me down with you,' he says. 'All you are is average. Average grades, average at sports, average at everything.'

I feel tears prickle the backs of my eyes. Chets never says anything mean about anyone unless they score higher than him in a maths test and then he gets a right strop on cos he hates not being the best at maths. He's never said anything this nasty to me before. I won't cry, though. Not in front of Katja. 'Why are you being like this?'

'Because I've had an awakening,' he says.

'I'm thinking this is either something to do with puberty or alien spores,' I say. 'Never thought I'd say this, but I'm hoping for puberty.'

'I've always been better than you.'

'You don't need to tell me that, Chets. I already know how special you are.'

'But you made me feel weak,' he says. 'When I ran into this shop earlier, I was scared and sad, and so very tired. But now I'm strong, and fast, and brave, and more powerful than you can possibly imagine.'

'Puberty, alien spores, puberty … Still can't tell.'

'When I left you,' he says, 'I was but the learner. Now I am the master.'

He takes off the sunglasses.

Katja gasps.

The centres of his eyes are black, ringed with bright yellow. Chets is an alien sporeling. And not just any sporeling – a hunter.

'Only a master of bug-eyes, Chets,' I say, backing towards the exit and thinking how this would be such a cool moment if my best friend hadn't just become a host to a parasitic alien.

'I'm so sorry this has happened to you. I really am,' I say, my brain racing.

'I'm not,' he says, stepping towards us. 'And when you become one of us you will understand.'

There's a moment of silence, filled with anticipation. Who moves first? Him? Me?

He leaps towards us, pulling back his head and making that flipping awful gurgling noise and the moment is gone. I pull over a bucket of Crater Lake frisbees and follow Kat through the shop. Chets trips on a frisbee and his spitball goes wide.

'I'll find a way to make this right,' I call over my shoulder.

'You won't get away,' he says. 'You'll turn. Everybody will. Our species will dominate this planet.'

We reach the door, throw it open and leg it to the lawn. There's no point trying to hide in the trees now, we just need to get to the lake. Chets is right on our tail. He seems faster than usual, and Kat and I are tired.

'Just a bit further, Katja,' I gasp. 'You need to try to go faster.'

'I can't,' she says. struggling through the tyres on the obstacle course.

I slow down, turn back to help her at the same time as Chets launches a giant spitball towards her. I try to shove her out of the way but it grazes her arm as it flies past. She retches like she's going to be sick but picks herself up and carries on running. Chets is gaining now. We're not going to make it.

14
An Unexpected Ally

I urge Katja forwards, knowing in my heart that Chets is going to catch us. Kat is slowing even more and I have to push her from behind. We're close to the lake but we're not going to get there.

I hear a shout, 'Out of my way, Chubs!' and a thud. I turn around and Trent is sprinting up behind us. 'They're after me,' he says.

The main entrance is flung open and Digger and Hoche come running across the lawn. Chets is rolling around on the ground.

'Chets!' I say. Idiot Trent must have shoved him out of the way in his desperation to escape. He's such a jerk.

'Leave him, he's done for,' Trent says. 'Where do we go?'

I hate Trent but I can't leave him to be alienated. 'The lake,' I say. 'We have to jump into the lake.'

'There they are,' Katja says, pointing to where

Big Mak and Adrianne are waving at us from the lake, holding on to a small raft with my backpack on it.

Kat is fading fast. Unnaturally fast.

'Into the water,' I yell, hoping it will wake her up a bit.

We leap in – Katja, Trent and me, and make for the others. Then we swim for our lives, pushing the raft in front of us. When I turn around I see Chets, Hoche and Digger standing on the pier, with all the worker bug-eyes behind them. They're not attempting to follow, which worries me as much as it cheers me.

We pull ourselves out of the water. Adrianne throws the backpack over her shoulders and Big Mak and I hold up Kat, half carrying her into the trees.

'Chets?' Mak says.

I shake my head.

'Chets is one of them?' Trent says.

'You mean you didn't know that when you pushed him out of the way?' I say. It's more of a statement than a question, though.

'If he's one of them, I probably just saved your lives. You should be thanking me.'

Trent is such a jerk.

'Great, we've lost a Chets and gained a Trent,' Adrianne says. 'And what happened to Katja?'

'The spit,' I say. 'I think it has something in it to make you sleep.'

'Like a sedative venom,' says Ade. 'That makes sense. That's why Digger was spitting into the water supply.'

'He probably spat in the tomato soup, too,' I gasp, while trying to stop Kat from falling to the ground.

'So glad we didn't eat that,' Mak says.

'Where are we going now?' Trent asks.

'I found a place. We'll have to circle back behind the building. We should be safe there for a while.' Mak stops for a moment. 'Wait a sec.'

'Are we ditching Katja?' Trent says. 'She's holding us back, and if she's going to fall asleep and turn into a bug-eye, we don't want her near us anyway.'

'We are not ditching Katja!' I turn on him. 'If you want to stick with us, Trent, you'd better stop being such a dirtbag.'

'Chill out, fangy. Just saying what everyone else was thinking.'

'None of us were thinking that, Trent,' Adrianne says.

'Right,' Mak says, putting Katja over his shoulder in some kind of highly impressive superhero carry. 'I can manage Kat. Let's get going.'

'Still with us, Kat?' I say.

She gives me a sleepy thumbs-up.

'If we can get her to basecamp before she goes out, we might be able to save her.'

We move out.

The new basecamp that Mak has picked out is closer to the building, but I'm thinking that could be a good thing because they won't think to look for us there. There's another hollowed-out bush – a bit thorny on the outside, so we can't get in without being scratched, but it feels safe on the inside.

'What can we do?' Adrianne says, taking off the backpack.

I grab the bag and unzip it, pulling out an oxygen tank which has a breathing mask attached to it by a tube.

'Put this over her mouth and nose,' I say, and

we secure it to her face, making sure the seal is tight to her skin, just as she stops responding.

I turn the valve on the neck of the tank, and hear the oxygen hissing up the tube and into the mask.

'Lance, you're a genius,' Adrianne says. 'If she's breathing pure oxygen, none of the spores should be able to get in.'

'We'll give her an hour's sleep, then try to wake her,' I say.

'What if it doesn't work?' asks Trent.

'It will work,' I say. 'And then we can take it in turns to have a sleep.'

'I dibs first go after Katja.'

Trent is such a jerk.

Mak goes into the new lookout tree, while Adrianne and I watch over Katja. She's sleeping peacefully and, as her wet hair dries in the sun, it forms little curls around her face. It makes her look younger.

Ade and I look through Dale's notes for more clues. We know what we're dealing with now, but what we don't know is how to stop the aliens. And as Chets is one of them, I'm desperate to find a way of turning him back.

'What happened in the dining hall?' I ask.

Trent talks through a mouthful of biscuit. 'It was fine. We were having a laugh, chilling out. We were going to settle down for some sleep but then we heard you over the speaker. We thought it wouldn't be a biggie, staying awake, but it got harder and harder. Then Miss Hoche started playing that music and tiredness just took over. I was alright, because obviously I'm a beast...'

Adrianne snorts.

'But the others were struggling. Imran and Isla fell asleep first.'

'Did you let them out like we said?' Adrianne asks.

'No way we were opening those doors,' Trent says. 'We tied them up with bag straps.'

'Then what happened?' I say.

'They went mental.' He shrugs. 'And we suddenly heard loads of noise coming from outside the dining hall. All the other bug-eyes were going at the doors with axes and hammers. They broke in and started rounding everyone up. I escaped.'

'Of course you did.' Adrianne rolls her eyes.

'What about the others?' I say.

'Dunno. Didn't stop to look. Every man for himself.' He stuffs another biscuit in his mouth.

'Nice,' I say.

'Don't judge me.' He spits crumbs at me. 'You let your best buddy Chets get buggy. You're no better.'

I bite my lip. There's no point arguing with Trent – he always has been and always will be a massive butt-brain. But I'm angry with myself, too, cos a little part of me knows there's some truth in what he's saying. It's my fault Chets became a bug-eye. And I have to fix it.

'It's been an hour,' Adrianne says. 'Shall we wake her?'

'It's just Katja, not flipping Sleeping Beauty,' Trent snorts, which just goes to show how stupid he is.

'Mak,' I call through the branches. 'We're going to wake her. Come down and get your stuff together, just in case.'

We pack up all our gear, tie our laces and put our bags on our backs.

'Ready?' I say.

They nod.

I kneel on the floor beside Kat and tap her gently on the arm.

'Katja?'

She doesn't respond.

I shake her shoulder, not too hard, and say her name again.

I think one of her eyelids moves a teeny tiny bit, but I can't be sure.

'Kat – I'm so sorry, but it's time to wake up.' This time I tap her arm with one hand and shake her shoulder with the other.

'For God's sake,' Trent says. Then he puts his face next to Katja's ear and screams, 'Aaarrgghhhhh!'

Kat sits bolt upright and gasps, the mask coming loose from her face. Her eyes open. They're the colour of a mystical lagoon where dolphins leap majestically and mermaids comb their hair.

'Katja, you're alright.' Adrianne squeaks and hugs her.

'What happened?' Kat says, squinting around at all of us.

'You took a hit in the arm,' I say. 'Chets' spit.'

'We think the hunters' spit contains a strong sedative,' says Ade.

Katja puts her hands to her face. 'I fell asleep!'

'But Lance got an oxygen mask on you first, so you didn't breathe in the spores,' says Mak.

'So I'm OK?'

'You're OK,' I say. And I smile for the first time in what feels like days, but is probably just hours.

15
Confession Time

We set Trent up with the oxygen and he crawls deeper into the hollowed-out bush to get some sleep.

He totally hasn't earned the right to have the next nap but, to be honest, we're all sick of listening to the rubbish that comes out of his stupid mouth and we're looking forward to some time to chat amongst ourselves without his smug comments.

Kat, Ade, Mak and I all climb up the lookout tree, and find the comfiest branches to sit on, which isn't easy cos branches weren't made to be comfortable for humans. We have Dale's notes with us but they're just a bunch of meaningless squiggles. They'd be hard to work out on a good day, but by now we're so tired we can't think straight – we've got no chance of getting anything useful from them.

'You feeling alright, Katja?' I ask.

'Surprisingly, I feel fine,' she says. 'Apart from the tiredness and hunger and blisters and stuff. How about you guys?'

'Same,' says Mak, yawning like a lion.

'Do you want the next sleeping slot?' I say.

'No, Adrianne should have it.'

'Why should I have it?' Adrianne says. 'Because I'm a girl?'

'Err…' Mak's stumped. I'm pretty sure there's no correct answer to this question.

'I'm not as tired as you so it makes sense that you go first,' she says. 'Unless you need to, Lance?'

'Nah, I'm OK. I'm used to managing on hardly any sleep. I mean, I'm tired, obviously, but I can wait a bit longer.'

'So is the CPAP machine yours?' Mak asks. I can't see him cos he's on a higher branch than me and hidden by the leaves, but I can hear in his voice that he's nervous about asking.

'How do you know about CPAPs?' I say.

'I've done a lot of first-aid training,' Mak says. 'Among other things.'

'What's a CPAP?' Kat asks. 'Is it that oxygen-mask thingy?'

'It's a breathing regulator,' says Mak. 'The

gadget attached to the tube makes sure the airways are kept open so breathing is stabilised. They're used by people with…'

'Sleep apnoea,' I say. This is part of the secret I've been holding so close for years. 'I have sleep apnoea. When I try to sleep, my breathing stops, then I jump awake. The hospital gave me the CPAP so I can get some proper rest. I can't sleep without it.'

'So that's why you never go to sleepovers?' Katja says.

'It's one of the reasons,' I say.

'What's the other reason?' Ade is up on the branch with Mak, and I imagine them looking at each other, making faces, raising eyebrows at Loser Lance and his weird sleeping habits. But I'm too tired and too much has happened for me to bother hiding stuff from them anymore.

'My mum has Crohn's disease.' I pick at my nails, which are black with dirt. 'She got it when she was pregnant with me. It makes her really sick. She goes into hospital a lot and she can't leave the house that much.'

'So you don't like people going to your house,' Mak says.

There's a moment of quiet.

'Why didn't you tell us?' Katja is sitting on the branch next to mine and I can tell she's looking right at me. I don't look back.

'Cos I didn't want to intimidate you with my coolness,' I say.

The branch above me rustles.

'Do you want to know how I know so much about first aid and survival skills and tracking?' Mak says.

'I've been wondering about that.' I risk a glance over at Kat. She smiles at me, and not in a weird way, in the same way she always does – like everything's safe and warm.

'You know how every summer I tell you I'm going to Lithuania to see my family, and I can't contact any of you because they don't have wifi?' Mak's family has been spending the whole summer in Lithuania for as long as I can remember.

'And you said nobody there has mobile phones,' says Kat.

'Yeah, well that's not strictly true,' says Mak. 'We do go to Lithuania, but not to see family. My mum and dad are preppers.'

'Preppers?' Adrianne says.

'They're getting me and Zuzie' (Zuzie is Mak's little sister) 'ready for the end of the world.'

'Wait ... what?' I've never heard Adrianne so confused.

'They think there's going to be a third world war, or a global natural disaster, or a zombie apocalypse, or some other massive event that will destroy the world as we know it,' Mak says. 'So they built a bunker in the countryside in Lithuania. It's, like, three storeys underground. It has electricity, a bathroom, kitchen, bedrooms. And it's full of stuff – everything we'd need to survive on our own for years. As far as bunkers go, it's legit.'

'So you go there every summer?' I say.

'Yeah, my parents take it super-seriously. We're totally off grid – not allowed any contact with the outside world. And they teach us to build fires and hunt and stuff.'

'Isn't Zuzie only in Reception?' Katja asks.

'Doesn't mean she can't snare a rabbit.'

'Wow,' says Ade.

'It must seem kind of insane to you guys,' Mak says.

Mak's parents seem so normal. I had no idea.

'Do you want to know why I'm so good at climbing?' I look over at Katja, but she's concentrating hard on braiding her hair.

'Err – yeah!' I say, because, let's face it – we've all been wondering.

'I was taken into care when I was really little,' she says. 'My mum couldn't look after me. She tried, but she couldn't.'

'Oh, Kat,' Adrianne says, 'I didn't know.'

'Nobody does.' Kat unbraids her hair and starts all over again. 'I was in a home for a while. It smelt funny and the bed was hard. My room felt like a prison. I hated it. So I ran away, over and over again. Then they put me in a foster home and I hated that, too. I got really good at climbing out of windows and escaping across rooftops.' She smiles in this way that makes her eyes twinkle. 'Eventually I went to a foster home I liked and my foster mum adopted me, so everything turned out fine. But, for a few years, climbing was the only thing that made me feel better.'

I really want to hug her, but that's not easy to do when you're perched on separate branches in a massive tree.

'I can't believe you guys have been keeping these huge secrets for so long,' Adrianne says. 'I mean, I would have thought you would have shared this stuff with each other. I understand why you wouldn't want it to be spread around the school, especially with idiots like Trent around.'

'So, what is the story with you two?' I say. 'We all thought you and Trent were besties, you know, being head boy and head girl together.'

'I've never liked him,' she says. 'I used to tolerate him, but then…'

'What happened?' Mak says.

'I don't want to say.'

'Please tell us, Ade,' Kat says. 'We've told you our secrets.'

'Tell us!' I say, and then we all start quietly chanting, 'Tell us, tell us, tell us.'

'Fine,' she says, 'but this story had better never leave this basecamp, or I will hunt you all down and kill you.'

'We promise,' I say. 'You can trust us.'

'It's not like the stuff you guys have been through,' she says. 'But it was the worst moment of my life. It happened in Year Five. It was half term and my mum got a call from Trent's mum saying he was having a last-minute birthday party, and that he'd really like me to go.'

'I don't remember him having a birthday party,' Mak says. 'I mean obviously we wouldn't have been invited…'

'…But he definitely would have made sure we knew about it.' One of Trent's favourite things was to make me, Chets, Mak and Kat feel left out.

'I didn't really want to go, but my mum made me feel guilty and said at least I'd get to see my friends, so I agreed,' Adrianne continues. 'Of course none of us had phones then, so I couldn't check with anyone.'

'I'm liking where this is going,' I say, and look over at Katja to see her grinning.

'So the next afternoon my mum drops me off at this posh spa hotel. Trent's mum meets us at the door and tells my mum to collect me at seven. That's five hours, I repeat, five hours from the time I got there. The first part of the party is in the pool, she says, so I get changed into my swimming things and go to the pool expecting everyone from school to be there.' She takes a breath. 'But there's just Trent and his entire family. Not just his mum and dad and older sister, but aunties and uncles and cousins. And me. I keep looking at the pool entrance, thinking any moment my friends are going to walk in. Or at least somebody I know. But an hour ticks by and I realise nobody else is coming. It's just me.'

'And the Trents,' Mak sniggers.

'I'm not happy about it, but I don't want to upset Trent's mum, so I just get on with it. Swim some laps. Play politely with the inflatables.'

'This is one of the best stories ever,' says Kat.

'Then, after swimming, we all get into the hot tub thing,' Ade says. 'And we sit in there, chatting, with these fruity drinks. All of us in a circle. I'm willing the time to pass quickly, but it feels like forever. Then finally we get out and get changed and everything.'

'Please say it's not over yet,' I say.

'It's not over yet,' Ade says, and I can imagine how pink her face is. 'We go into the hotel restaurant and they've booked a huge table for all of them, and it's decorated with balloons and sparkles and birthday banners. I go to sit down, but the waiter says, "*Non, mademoiselle*, we have a special table for the birthday boy and his girlfriend".'

Kat lets out a little squeak of giggle and I squeeze my lips shut tight so I don't laugh.

'Next to the big table,' Ade says, 'is another small table, with two chairs…' She pauses.

'Go on,' Mak says.

Another breath. 'And a … rose. And a candle.'

Katja is shaking with giggles she's trying not to let out. I put a twig in my mouth and bite down hard. Anything to keep from laughing. Mak makes a noise that is half laugh, half cough.

'The whole family is saying how sweet it is and taking photos of us. "Hold hands!" they say, and I'm dying inside and I wish I had drowned in the swimming pool.'

There's no holding it in now, we're laughing so hard we nearly fall out of the tree.

'It was harrowing,' Ade says.

'What did you do?' Mak asks.

'I got up and ran to the reception of the hotel and started crying.' Even Adrianne is laughing now. 'Trent's mum called my mum to pick me up and I sobbed all the way home.'

We laugh so much that the whole tree shakes and bits of leaf and twig drop through the branches like confetti.

'We'd better wake Trent up,' I say. 'We don't know how long we'll have here before the bug-eyes come, and we all need to get some sleep.'

'Maybe he's been eaten by bears,' Ade says, hopefully.

'Dale said something about bears, remember?' I say. 'Right after he asked for water. I wonder what that was about.'

Kat gasps and starts flicking through Dale's notes. 'I saw something – a picture,' she says. 'Here it is!'

She leans over and shows me a pencil sketch of a creature that looks like a cross between a woodlouse and a hippo. Underneath is written WATER BEAR, and it's underlined about eight times.

'What the hell's a water bear?' I say.

'It's another name for a tardigrade,' Mak calls down. 'Let me see the pic.' A hand is thrust down through the leaves. I pass him the bit of paper.

'Yeah, this is a tardigrade,' he says.

'It looks terrifying,' says Adrianne. 'I hope there aren't any lurking around here.'

'First of all, they're tiny,' says Mak. 'You can only see them through a microscope, kind of like the alien spores. And, second, they're actually awesome. They can survive the most extreme conditions and they live off stuff that would kill other species. They eat the bad bits of things, the rotten parts, and leave the healthy parts behind – like they can purify water, for example.'

'OK, this is interesting.' My brain is fighting through its sleepy fog, but I'm sure there's something here we can use.

'Guys,' Adrianne says, and a branch above me creaks. I think she's climbing higher up the tree. 'I see movement. Can you get any higher, Kat?'

Katja leaps up the trunk and out of my view like some kind of tree-climbing ballerina. 'It's them,' she says. 'Hoche, Digger and Chets. They're spread out through the trees and heading this way.'

'Damn, they're sweeping the woods,' I say. 'Everyone climb down as quickly and quietly as possible. We'll grab our stuff and move on.'

'We'd better wake Trent,' Kat says.

'Or we could leave him?' Adrianne climbs down to my branch and then drops to the ground. 'Ew, bird poo,' she says, and wipes her hands on Trent's backpack.

16
Back in the Hive

Two minutes later, we're trekking through the trees again.

'Where are we going now?' Trent says. He wasn't happy about being woken up and I genuinely think he would have refused to take off the oxygen mask if we hadn't told him the hunters were on their way.

'I've been thinking,' I say. 'Everyone except us has been alienated now, right? And they think we're hiding in the woods.'

'So we go back into the building?' says Ade.

'The centre is clear as far as they're concerned. The security cameras are off, thanks to Chets. I don't think they'll look for us there.'

'Are you mental?' Trent says, far too loudly considering we're being hunted by hostile aliens. 'I'm not going back to that place.'

'You don't have to,' Adrianne says. 'You can stay outside on your own.'

'It's a good idea, Lance. We can hole up, get a bit more rest.' Mak really seems to be struggling – he can hardly keep his eyes open.

'And we can get a closer look at what they're up to down there,' says Ade.

'Who cares what they're up to?' Trent says. 'All we have to do is keep out of their way for one more night. The coach will be back tomorrow morning and we can get the hell out of here.'

'It can't hurt to do some more recon.' I don't have the energy to argue about this with Trent. Why does he have to make everything so hard? 'Our friends have turned into alien bugs. Don't you want to be able to help them once we get out of here?'

He just shrugs.

'Nice,' Kat says.

'You're willing to sacrifice yourself to save the rest of the class?' Trent says. 'Then you're idiots.'

'We're not idiots, Trent. We just want to do what's right,' I say.

'Yeah, you're so perfect, aren't you, Fangs? Wouldn't ever do anything horrible to anyone, like shut them in the toilets so they miss their Bing entrance exam?'

'Shut up, Trent,' I say.

'Still haven't told them?' He smirks in his infuriating way. 'I thought you were all such good friends.'

I'm scared to tell them because of the way Chets reacted, but I'm so sick of this hanging over my head. It's been nine months of lying. Nine months of being afraid that the truth will come out. And I'm done with it.

'Fine,' I say. 'I did trap you in the toilets, Trent. And if I was in that situation again, I'd do the same thing.'

'Finally! I'm telling Miss Hoche, if she ever stops being an alien.'

'I told her this morning,' I say. 'And I'll take whatever punishment she gives me.'

'Is that what you and Chets argued about?' Kat says.

I nod. We've stopped walking and are standing in a circle in a small clearing in the trees.

'Why did you shut him in?' Kat says, and I'm surprised because nobody's ever seemed to care about why someone trapped Trent in the toilets, only that someone (aka me) did and that it was a despicable thing to do.

'Because I didn't want him to get into Bing,' I say. 'I was in the toilets and I heard him talking to his mates.'

Trent looks down and starts scuffing his feet in the dry dirt.

'He said that Bing is going to be ultra-competitive. That he'll have to go in hard and prove himself if he wants to be top dog. He's planning to use Chets to make his point – he's going to make Chets' life miserable so that everyone knows he's not weak.'

I realise I'm breathing fast and my heart is thumping in my chest. I feel like I might faint.

'He said that with me out of the way, he'll be able to do whatever he wants to Chets. Because I won't be there to protect him.'

'Did you tell Chets that?' Mak says.

'No, not that part. He's super-excited about going there, and he should be – he's so smart. I didn't want to ruin it for him – to make him scared before he's even started.'

'Why didn't you admit it was you straight away, though?' Mak says. 'You don't normally lie about stuff.'

'Because Hoche already had it in for me. If she

171

knew I did it, she would have excluded me. Then I wouldn't be with any of you guys and I wouldn't be able to keep Chets safe.'

'When Chets stops being an alien, you need to explain this to him,' Kat says. 'He'll forgive you, I know he will.'

'And what about you guys?' I say. 'Do you hate me?'

'I do,' Trent says.

'Well, that's no loss,' Adrianne says. 'I don't hate you, Lance. I don't think you went about things in the best way, but I can understand anyone wanting to shut Trent away in a room.'

'I'd probably have done the same thing if I'd have been there,' Mak says. 'Or possibly something worse.'

'You did it for the right reasons, Lance.' Katja puts her arm around me. She smells of coconut cupcakes and warm milk. 'You're a good friend.'

And just like that, the secret that's been burning a hole in me for months is out. And my friends are still my friends. Well, except Chets, but I'm going to make that right.

'Thanks, guys,' I say, and I take a stupidly long time rooting around in my bag for my water, even though I know it's in the back pocket, cos I don't want them to see how close I am to crying.

'Unbelievable,' says Trent, and he storms off ahead.

It isn't long before we can see the roof of the centre through the trees. Trent crashes towards it like a hungry T-Rex chasing its prey.

'I'd say our chances of surviving are significantly lower with him around,' Adrianne says.

As we get closer, I realise something big is going down at the lake. There's a lot of noise – like at the dam site but times a hundred. We're at the back of the building, so we can't see what's going on, but whatever it is, it's keeping the bug-eyes busy, so we can sneak in without being seen.

Our priority right now is getting Mak set up with the CPAP. He looks like hell – his eyes are red, the skin around them a worrying grey colour. We make our way to my room, which is exactly as I left it, fit the mask to his face and switch on the machine. He lies on the bed, and is asleep in literally three seconds. It's weird seeing him like this. He's the biggest of all of us, and with his shaved hair and muscles, he usually seems so tough. Now he looks like any other kid, all tuckered out after a long day.

'So what now?' Kat says.

'We need to find out what's happening by the lake,' I say.

'Trent and I should go as we've both had some sleep. You and Adrianne can wait here and chill.'

'I'm not going out there.' Trent is sitting on the floor and has got out a pack of cards. He doesn't even look up.

Adrianne opens her mouth to argue with him, but I stop her. 'To be honest,' I say, 'I'd rather do something. Keep moving. If I sit down, I might pass out.'

'Same,' Ade says.

'OK.' Kat sits down and leans back against the bed. 'I'll stay and watch Mak. Be careful, guys.'

'You too,' I say. 'And if anything goes wrong, feel free to sacrifice Trent.'

17
Stuff Gets Bad

Ade and I decide to leave the building by the back entrance and make our way round to the lake from the outside. It's late afternoon and there's no breeze to relieve the scorching heat. The air smells stale, like last week's PE kit, and my skin itches.

We edge around the red brick wall, past the security office and the fire exit, until we have a good view of the lake, or what's left of it.

'They are draining it,' Adrianne says. 'Look, they've dug a channel that leads out of the crater for the water to run down.'

'I think that's a pump they have running, too.'

'So what do you think happens when the lake is empty?' she asks.

'We know they hate the water,' I say. 'It's too cold for them. But it's a lot of trouble to go to when they could easily just avoid going in there.'

'So you think there's another reason.'

'It's the only thing that makes sense. They're

trying to accomplish something, and emptying the lake is part of it.'

'But what, though?'

'The end of the world?' I say.

Ade looks at me. 'Are you thinking what I'm thinking?'

'We need more information.'

'Agreed.'

'Are you up for getting a bit closer?' I say.

She's running for the treeline without bothering to answer. You have to respect her conviction – she's a girl who gets things done. I guess there are pros and cons to this alien-invasion business, but one major bonus has been spending time with Adrianne. All those years at school together, and I never really knew her at all. Life or death dramas are great for bonding, apparently. Who knew?

We use the trees as cover and make our way around the main clearing to a place where the lake comes closest to the trees, separated only by a path just wide enough for cars to drive down. To our right is a biggish building, kind of like an upgraded garden shed, or one of those creepy barns in movies where the murderer keeps his victims tied up. The grass surrounding it is long, dead-looking and full of buzzing insects. There are tyre tracks leading from the road, through the yellow grass, to the giant front door which is open a crack, so I reckon the staff keep their cars parked in there.

We drop to our bellies and slither through the grass like snakes, only less stealthy and with more under-breath swears as we get scratched and bitten by insects. We stop at the side of the serial-killer shed, and watch and listen.

'See how low the water level is already?' I say. It's at least a metre lower than it was when we swam it earlier. That lake saved us, and now it's disappearing scarily fast.

Ade doesn't answer, so I look over and I see that she's dozing off.

'Ade,' I whisper, scared to give away our position.

Her head starts to droop forward.

I nudge her hard in the side with my elbow.

She jumps awake with a yelp that sounds like the noise my cat makes when you stand on her tail. A group of bug-eyes standing by the road all turn to look in our direction. We flatten ourselves down into the crispy grass and I hold my breath, not that that's going to make a difference.

Two of the bug-eyes start walking our way.

'The shed,' I say. I don't want to go in there, but there's no time to hide anywhere else. The bug-eyes are a little way off and the front of the shed is angled away from them, so there's a chance we might make it.

We belly wriggle towards the door, open it just wide enough to squeeze through, and then pull it almost shut behind us.

'Can you see anything, owl-eyes?' I ask Adrianne. It's so dark in here, visibility is pretty much zero.

'Not much, but there's something big over there. I think it's a van or something – we should hide underneath it in case they come in.'

She's right. I know she's right. But there's something about this shed that gives me the proper creeps. Going deeper in is like swimming inside a shark's jaws. It can only end badly.

She grabs my arm and leads me through the darkness. I can just about make out the van she was talking about, though it's covered in a cloth or a tarp or something. We feel our way around and crawl underneath. Just in time.

The shed door is pulled open about a metre,

and through the weave of the tarp I see sunlight flood in. I edge forwards to take a peek. If they find us under here, we have nowhere to run, so it's pretty risky. But we can't waste an opportunity to find out more about what's going on.

A bug-eye walks through the open door. It's not one of the hunters. I think it might be Krish. There's another bug-eye behind, but he's looking the other way so I can only see the back of him. It looks like the same guy that Hoche had tied to the chair in the office.

'There doesn't appear to be anything out of place out here,' chair guy says.

'It's possible the noise was an animal, but we must be cautious.' The other bug-eye is definitely Krish. He's gazing around the shed. I don't think I've ever held my body so still – it's almost painful. 'This stage of the incursion is vital. The lake must be emptied. We cannot be delayed.'

'But we are on course,' says chair guy. 'The lake will be drained by sunrise, the sun's heat will reach our brothers and sisters who have been trapped under that repulsive water for so many years. Then they will be free to fly and find new bodies to take root in.'

'It will be liberating to leave the confines of this crater,' says Krish.

'Nothing will stop us.' Chair guy turns around and my heart almost bursts out of my chest.

'I see nothing unusual here,' says Krish. 'Let us get back to work.'

The two bug-eyes leave the shed.

My heart is pounding and my mouth dry. We wait a minute before moving. Then we inch out from our hiding place.

'Ade,' I say. 'Did you recognise that bug-eye? The older guy?'

'There was something familiar about him,' she says, 'but I can't work out where I know him from.'

I swallow. Take a breath. 'I think it was the driver.'

'Our driver?'

'Yes, the one who's supposed to be collecting us tomorrow morning.'

'OK, this is bad.' She balls her hands into fists and rubs her eyes with her knuckles. 'Does that mean the coach isn't coming back?'

I take hold of the tarp and pull it with all of my strength. Through the light coming in from the open door, we get a good look at what's underneath. It's the coach.

I feel tired, empty and sick. 'I don't think it ever left.'

18
At Last

We get back to my room to find Mak awake and looking a lot better.

'You go next, Adrianne,' I say.

She smiles at me and flops on to the bed without saying anything. She puts on the mask and rolls over to face the wall. A minute later her breathing gets slower and deeper. She's asleep.

'What happened?' Kat says. 'I'm assuming it's not good news.'

I look at Trent. 'Before I tell you, I want everyone to stay calm. We need to be quiet. We need to think carefully. Nobody panic.'

'Spit it out, man,' Trent says. 'What's the beef?'

''K. Well, the good news is that we found out why the bug-eyes are draining the lake. The bad news is that it's so they can free the rest of the alien spores and take over the world.'

'We figured it was something like that, anyway,' Mak says. 'So it's good to have official confirmation.'

'Yeah, Fangs – what's the big deal? When the coach comes tomorrow, we escape, call the police, the police sort it out and we get the credit. Simples.' Trent tosses a handful of Starmix into his mouth.

'The big deal...' I say, and I'm thinking that, if I say it really quick, it won't sound as bad '...is that the coach driver's a bug-eye, the coach is hidden in a murder-y barn by the lake and, if we don't stop the bug-eyes by sunrise, then it's probably going to be too late.'

Trent swallows the candies whole. It sounds like a dog choking on a chicken carcass.

'So we're on our own?' Katja says.

'Well, not completely,' I say. 'We've got each other.'

'Hell, yeah!' says Mak. 'I'd trust you guys with my life over anyone else in the world.'

'You're all mental.' Trent's stopped choking and is knocking back a bottle of Evian. 'I'd rather be with a pack of velociraptors than you lot.'

'So what's the plan?' Katja asks.

'We have to stop the lake from being drained,' I say. 'Mak, do you think there's any way we can break down that dam?'

'The thing with dams,' he says, munching on what looks like bits of twig, 'is you don't need to break the whole thing down; you only need to make a crack in the right place.'

'So it's do-able?'

'They put it up in a hurry. It's not structurally sound. It's definitely do-able.'

'But how are we going to get it done with so many bug-eyes around?' Kat says. 'There's too many of them.'

'I've got a couple of ideas,' I say. 'But nothing substantial enough that I can feel sure it will work.'

I rub my hands through my hair so hard I think I may have left a bald patch. I'm so tired – it's like nothing I've ever felt before. I miss my mum. I miss Chets. I feel like the fate of the human race depends on me, and my brain and body are just shutting down.

'We have some time, Lance,' Kat says. 'When Adrianne wakes up you can sleep. After that, things will seem better. We'll think of something.'

I want to believe her, but it all seems too much. I came on this trip to protect Chets. I failed. I tried to stop everybody from turning into aliens. I failed. I fail at everything – at school, at home and in life. All I want to do is go to sleep, drift off to a happy place and forget about it.

'We wouldn't have got this far without you,' Kat says, like she's reading my mind.

'We'd have been toast on the first night,' says Mak. 'RIP us.'

'I'd have been fine,' Trent says. Kat hits him in the face with a towel.

'Here, eat a banana.' Mak passes one to me. 'Thirty minutes, then it's your turn to sleep. And, honestly, mate, that hour of sleep is gonna make you feel unstoppable.'

'And tomorrow, when we're home, we can all sleep for a week,' Kat says. 'They'll let us have a couple of days off school, right?'

Somehow the others keep me awake until it's my turn with the CPAP. I feel weird cos I never sleep in front of anyone, but there have been a lot of firsts on this trip, so I guess one more won't hurt. As I put the mask over my nose and mouth, I worry for a second that I'm too wired to sleep – that the stress and craziness will keep me up, worrying. But I only worry for a second, and then

I fall into a heavy black cloud, where nothing matters except the steady beat of my heart.

I wake to see Katja gazing down at me, the turquoise of her eyes twinkling like a mythical jewel from Asgard or something.

'How are you feeling?' she asks.

'Better,' I say. Part of me wants to let myself slide back into sleep, but I know I've got stuff to do; the others are counting on me. So I sit up and take off the mask. 'Where's that page of notes about water bears? I've had an idea.'

'Geek, Robot, Overlord for the next turn?' Trent dangles the oxygen mask in his hand.

'Just shut up and go to sleep, if you don't want to help,' Adrianne says.

'Don't come crying to me later, saying I didn't give you a fair chance then.' Trent jumps on to the bed and settles down for another nap.

'Here's the page you wanted, Lance.' Katja hands me a crumpled piece of paper. 'I think it looks more like a hippo than a bear.'

'What do you know about tardigrades, Mak?' I say.

'They're tiny. They survive in conditions that

nothing else can deal with – they can even come back from the dead. They can stand boiling hot, freezing cold, total dehydration and being in space. They eat all sorts of stuff, including bacteria, which is why they can be useful.'

'Is it possible they could eat alien bacteria?' I ask, looking at the creature in the diagram.

'I guess it's possible,' Mak says. 'You could be on to something.'

'But where can we get some?' Katja asks. 'We don't have access to shops here.'

'They often live in green or watery places. Another name for them is moss piglets.'

'Remember just before Dale passed out – he said something about water bears and he had green slime on him?' I say. 'I reckon there are tardigrades in the crater somewhere. That's what he was trying to find when he bugged out.'

'The moss!' Kat widens her eyes to infinity-pool proportions. 'There's moss around the edge of the crater. Chets slipped in some on the way in.'

'Maybe the moss has been helping to keep the spores from escaping the crater,' Ade says.

We look at each other and I'm sure they're all thinking what I'm thinking – that this could be the key to stopping the aliens. It's an epic moment, full of possibility and hope. Then Trent farts in his sleep.

'Alright,' I say. 'I have a plan. It's all based on guesswork and assumptions, so there's a high chance of it going wrong.'

'I'm in,' says Katja.

'Me too,' says Adrianne.

'Of course, I'm totally in.' Mak grins. 'And I hope it involves getting out of this room because if Trent farts again, I might be sick.'

'Right.' I jump up and I'm feeling full of energy again. Nothing makes you feel worse than running away and hiding from things. When you make the decision to face them and fight them, even though it's scary, it's like the dark clouds blow away and everything becomes clear.

'Empty your backpacks, except for water and a snack. We're going to forage for some moss.'

'What about Trent?' Kat says. 'Should we wake him?'

'Nah. He made his choice. Leave him here to sleep.'

Five minutes later, we're leaving the building through the back entrance and making our way into the trees. It feels good to be doing something useful, and with my best friends beside me. I only wish Chets could be here, too.

'So we know there's some moss by the main gate,' I say. 'But the main gate is risky – they could be watching it.'

'Let's start at this side and work our way around the crater,' Katja says, skipping up the savagely steep slope as though she's on flat ground.

The rest of us follow as best we can, though by the time we see the fence through the trees, we're practically climbing. A few metres before the fence, Kat suddenly stops and wobbles as though she's on the edge of something. Adrianne is second in line and just about manages to grab Kat's backpack and keep her from falling. As Mak and I catch up, I see that where Kat and Ade are standing, there's a deep dip in the earth, with vertical sides, laced with bits of dead root. It's like the ground has been ripped out. On the other side of the ditch, the fence rises ominously.

'It looks like someone's dug a trench,' says Mak.

'To stop us from getting out?' Adrianne asks.

Katja stands with her hands on her hips, assessing the vertical sides of the trench. 'I can climb that, no problem. But I don't think you guys will be able to. No offence.'

As if anyone could ever be offended by something that Katja says.

'Lucky we're not here to try to climb our way out,' I say. 'But if there was any moss there, it's long gone.'

'So we follow the perimeter?' says Mak.

'Yes,' I say. 'Maybe the ditch is only across the back of the crater.'

We trudge on, keeping the ditch on our right. It's strange to see the world outside the fence, going on exactly as it did before. Life in the crater is so disconnected, we might as well be on an alien planet.

'Remember when Chets thought there were bandits in the woods?' I say, and we all laugh, until we remember there are nastier things to worry about than bandits.

'So I guess Digger hit Dale on the head to try to knock him out,' says Ade. 'That's one way of making someone sleep.'

'Or killing them,' says Mak.

'And after everything he went through, they got him anyway.' I can't see Kat's face cos she's walking ahead of me, but I know she hates seeing people get hurt. Since we came across the ditch it's like everyone's spirits are falling again.

'If we can find the moss and fix this,' I say, 'then nothing Dale went through will be wasted. If he hadn't left the notes, or scared the butts off us by smearing his blood over the coach window, we never would have known what we were dealing with. I mean we've worked some things out for ourselves, but a lot of it is cos of his lunatic scribbles. We won't let his sacrifice be in vain.'

Katja sniffs.

'That was rousing, mate,' Mak says and he pretends to break down in tears. 'Especially the part about Dale's blood smears.'

Ade starts giggling and whacks Mak on the arm. 'It was a good speech, Lance. You really should have run for head boy.'

'I'd have voted for you,' says Kat.

'Me too. And Chets,' Mak says.

'Yeah, I don't think three votes would have won it for me, but thanks anyway, guys.'

'If more people had really got to know you,

things could have been different,' Adrianne says. 'We've been in the same class for years, seen each other nearly every day, but all I knew about you was that your attendance is in the low eighties, you find it hard to concentrate, you don't seem to care about the SATS or doing well, and sometimes you get into trouble. You've kept so much to yourself and allowed people to think the worst of you.'

'It kind of suited me to be seen as the class idiot. It meant nobody bothered asking questions,' I say, and I realise that I've actually been quite a coward. I took what seemed like the easiest option: the least risky way of getting through. Maybe I was wrong.

'If people knew about your mum, and about your other difficulties, sure there would be a few jerks like Trent who'd laugh and say horrid things, but most people would be nice about it,' Ade says. 'You should have given us a chance.'

'And I can't believe you didn't tell *us*,' says Katja. 'We're your best friends, Lance. We know how awesome you are.'

'Hey – we've all kept things to ourselves, buddy.' Mak whacks me gently on the back of my shoulder. 'Even the girls.'

There's a few seconds of quiet – no sound but our footsteps.

'Yeah, we did both do that, too, Ade,' says Kat, and then she starts giggling.

'You're thinking about that little table in the restaurant, aren't you?' Ade says.

'And the rose,' Mak splutters.

I can barely hold in the laughter. 'Don't forget the candle.'

We all laugh so hard that we have to stop walking. There's so much going on and things are looking pretty bad right now, as our only plan seems to have been dug up and thrown away, but it feels amazing to laugh like this. We give it a few minutes, holding our bellies and falling to the ground. Then Katja snorts and Big Mak starts crying, and we start all over again. We laugh until we ache, and I know that whatever happens, however it all turns out, this is one of the best moments of my life.

'If I live to be an old man, I'm going to sit at bus stops, telling people this story,' I say. 'It's never going to stop being funny.'

'We'll all live in the same old people's home,' says Kat. 'We can talk about it while we do our knitting.'

'I'm an excellent knitter,' Mak says. 'It's one of the life-skills my parents taught me.'

And we all laugh again.

After a water and wee break, we continue our walk around the crater of doom. The ditch doesn't let up, but we have to keep hoping.

'It's gonna be by the road,' I say. 'They won't have dug it up cos they need it for getting in and out. That's where we'll find the moss.'

And as we approach the only road through the crater, we can see that it's intact.

'There are guards,' Mak says.

'Of course there are,' I sigh. No way are they going to make this really hard thing we have to do any easier for us. 'How many?'

Mak crawls forward for a better look. 'Just two. Crater Lake guys.'

'They're making sure nobody gets out of the gate, I guess,' Kat says. 'What are we going to do?'

'They're only workers – let's take them out. We'll grab some branches and hit them round the head.' Mak starts scoping the trees for a suitable weapon.

'Too risky,' I say. 'They're bigger than us and we

won't be able to sneak up on them so we won't have the element of surprise.'

'Besides,' says Ade, 'remember the aliens have displayed wasp-like tendencies so far. If we attack one of the hive, they'll release the pheromone that alerts all of the others. We're out in the open here. The pheromone will spread quickly and there'll be a swarm.'

'We have to lure them away, and there's only one way I can think of.' I roll my shoulders back and do some warm-up stretches.

'We're not using you as bait,' says Kat. 'It's too dangerous.'

'It's the only way,' I say. 'I'll draw them away and you guys get as much moss as you can.'

'The problem with this plan is that you're too slow.' Adrianne stands up and tightens her ponytail. 'So I'm being the bait.'

'I can't ask you to do that,' I say.

'You're not asking, I'm volunteering. It's the option that has the greatest chance of success. I'm the fastest, so I'll go.'

'No way. It's not happening.' It's so dangerous. The thought of watching Ade run into the jaws of death is too awful for me to deal with. It should be me.

'It isn't your choice to make,' she says. 'It's not your job to protect everyone all the time – you have to let us take responsibility for ourselves. I'm the fastest, so this makes the most sense.'

I can see that she's determined, and she's right – it does make the most sense. She's way faster than me. But still…

'I'll Geek, Robot, Overlord you for it?' I say.

'Did it ever cross your mind that you're not actually helping people by protecting them all the time?' she asks. 'Take Chets, for example. You saved him from the wasp. You got stung. He didn't. And are you scared of wasps now?'

'No,' I say.

'And is Chets still scared of wasps?'

'Hell, yes,' says Mak.

'Exactly. Sometimes the fear of something happening is worse because you've never experienced it before. Once it's happened to you and you've got through it, you realise it's not so bad.'

'You're saying Chets might be less scared of wasps if I'd let him get stung?'

'It's possible,' she says.

'Ade, you're blowing my mind,' says Kat.

'Group vote then,' Adrianne says. 'Everyone in favour of me luring the bug-eyes away from the gate, raise your hands.'

Kat sticks her hand up with an unhappy look on her face. Adrianne glares at Big Mak and he puts his hand up too. I give him a look but he shrugs. 'She's like a flipping cheetah, mate. You're more like a ferret or something.'

'I win, three to one,' she says. 'I can do this. Trust me.'

I nod. 'Be careful.'

'Run fast, Ade.' Katja hugs her.

And she's gone, running noisily through the trees and on to the road in front of the two bug-eyes, where she fake trips and falls to the ground. She looks up and pretends to be surprised when she sees the guards. It's hard to tell what the guards are thinking at this point, cos their eyes are just bottomless dark and their faces expressionless. But it only takes a couple of breaths for them to launch into action. They move towards Ade. She lets them come for a few steps, then she jumps up and darts into the trees on the other side of the road, without looking back.

'Respect.' Mak sighs – his eyes all big and gooey.

'Let's move,' I say, and we make for the gate.

'There's moss, lots of it,' Katja says, as we get close. We pull our bags off our backs and start unzipping them as we run. There's no way of knowing how long we'll have before the guards come back, or are replaced by some other bug-eyes.

We reach the mounds of moss, scrape it up with our hands and cram it into the backpacks. It's only when we've taken nearly all of it, that I look up and notice. 'The gate's open.'

19
A Chance to Escape

'The lock must have deactivated when Chets hacked the security system,' I say, gently pushing the gate cos I can't quite believe we have a way out right here, right in front of us. 'One of you should go – it's a long way back to civilization, but you might be able to get help.'

'But we need all three of us to carry out the rest of the plan,' Katja says. 'It can't work with two people, especially now Ade has gone.'

'But they won't know you've gone,' I say to Kat. 'They won't be looking for you out there. It's a chance to get away from this damn crater – we might not get another one.'

'No,' she says. 'I'm not going. We'll find another way.'

'Mak?' I turn to him.

'Like Kat says, we'll find another way. Anyway, I'm not leaving this place without you guys, Adrianne and Chets.'

'And if we don't stop the aliens, it won't be any safer out there anyway,' says Kat.

We look out at the road stretching through the trees, away from the crater, away from the bug-eyes, towards home and our parents and air conditioning. Then we gather up the rest of the moss and race back into the woods, towards the centre.

We make it back with no sign of Adrianne or any of the bug-eyes. We're all quiet. Focussed. With Adrianne and Chets gone, our group feels small and stuff is starting to get real.

Trent is still asleep on the bed when we open the door to my room.

'Chets is a gross, spitty, hunter thing, Adrianne is running through the woods being chased by bug-eyes, the rest of our class have been body-snatched by aliens, and he's just sleeping,' Kat says. It's the closest to angry I've ever seen her.

'It's going to be dark in a couple of hours,' I say, looking at my useless phone. It still has fifty per cent power left – funny how long the battery lasts when you can't actually use it for anything. 'We should wake him and see if he'll help.'

'Ooh, I'll wake him,' Mak says, pulling a bottle of water out of his bag.

As much as I'd like to throw a whole flipping bucket of water over Trent, now isn't the time. 'Gently, Mak – we can't have him shouting out.'

'Spoilsport,' he says, and he walks over to the bed.

'So what now?' asks Katja.

'We need to test this moss – see if the tardigrades have any effect on the bug-eyes.' I've thought about this, and there's something I want to try. It's not the most sensible plan I've ever had. It's possibly the most stupidly dangerous plan I've ever had. But I want to try. 'We're going to trap a bug-eye and run some experiments.'

'But what about the pheromones?' Mak sits down on the floor with us, leaving Trent to whine in the corner about how rude we are to wake him up.

'If we enclose the bug-eye immediately, before he gets a chance to sound the alarm, we should be able to stop the pheromones from reaching the other aliens,' I say.

'You're calling the bug-eye "him",' Kat says. 'You've already decided who we're going after, haven't you?'

'Yep. We're going to get Chets and we're going to make him human again.'

'You're mental,' Trent says. 'If you're crazy enough to try to abduct an alien, you should at least go for one of the stupid worker ones.'

'But strategically it could be a good call,' I say. 'We'd be taking one of the hunters out of the mix, which is going to be a massive help when we instigate the endgame. Chets is the smallest and he hasn't been turned for as long as the others, so he probably has the least sporiness about him.'

'Also, he's our best mate, jerk-face,' Mak says, looking at Trent in disgust. 'If there's any chance we can turn him back, then obviously we have to try.'

'How are you going to turn him back?' Trent snorts. 'Expelliarmus?'

'With this moss,' says Kat, holding open her backpack for him to see. 'We think there are tiny creatures called water bears living in it, and that they will eat the alien virus.'

'Where's Adrianne?' he says, looking around like he's just noticed she's not there, which is typical Trent cos he's so self-obsessed.

'She led the bug-eyes away from the gate so we could collect the moss,' Mak says.

'Why are there bug-eyes at the gate? Surely they know we're not going to be able to climb over?'

Trent says. 'And there's all that thorny wire at the top of them. Nobody's getting out that way.'

'The gates are open,' says Kat.

'What do you mean?'

'The gates aren't locked. So they're guarding them.'

'Hold up a bit,' Trent says. 'Are you saying that you were at the gates, the gates were open, the guards were gone and you didn't try to escape?'

'There are more important things,' I say. 'We're not leaving anyone behind.'

'I always knew you were a bunch of weirdos, but this is a new level of idiotness.' Trent tucks into a chocolate bar and laughs to himself.

We turn away and ignore him.

'So how do we get to Chets?' Kat says.

From the security-room window, Katja, Big Mak and I have a good view across the lawn to the lake. Pretty much all the bug-eyes are out there, disappearing into the tunnel they're digging to channel the water from the lake, or operating the generator and pump. The lake is visibly shrinking now. We need to hurry.

The hunters seem to have given up combing

the woodland for us. Instead they're circling the site, looking out into the trees, alert for any signs of life. It's like they know that once the lake has been drained the spores will catch up with us, so they're focusing all their efforts on the main act.

Lucky for us, Digger, Hoche and Chets are separate, spaced out around the circumference of the lake. I could be imagining it, or my eyes might have gone nuts due to lack of sleep, but they look different to me. Especially Digger. He was big before but it's like he's grown taller and broader, and he's slightly hunched over, like there's something up with his back. He's too far away to see properly, so I put it out of my mind and laser my thoughts on to our plan. All we have to do is draw Chets away without him raising the alarm. Easy, right?

We make our way as stealthily as we can into the trees and through the woods to the area Chets is guarding. We take our positions. Adrianne still hasn't returned and Trent refused to help with our quote 'suicide mission', so it's just the three of us. But hopefully that's all we'll need.

Mak, who apparently is an expert in imitating bird noises, makes a low whistling sound. It sounds strange in the silence of the woods. The only wildlife we've heard since we got here has been the insects. All the other birds and animals seem to have cleared out.

Chets' head jerks up and he scans the treeline.

Mak whistles again.

Chets moves towards the tree where Mak is hiding.

This is Kat's signal to move. As Chets stalks closer to Mak's tree, a light thud comes from another tree further in. Kat has played her move perfectly, throwing a rock against a rotten trunk. Nothing too loud but enough to lure Chets away from Mak's hiding place.

When Chets reaches the tree, he finds a sweet wrapper. And not just any sweet wrapper – a green Maoam stripe, which he knows is my favourite.

We gradually move him through the trees, leaving a trail of noises and clues, Hansel and Gretel style. We try to play it out like it's not deliberate, making some of the breadcrumbs hard to find, like we've tried to conceal them.

This game is all about patience.

Eventually we get him into the building and to the kitchen door.

Chets doesn't hesitate, throwing the door open and making for the fridge. We've left the fridge door open a crack and, from where I'm hiding, I see Chets' weird bug face light up as he realises he has us trapped.

He pulls the door open and peers inside.

Big Mak and me are inside the fridge, our backs against the wall on either side of the door.

'Now!' I shout. We both grab an arm and pull Chets into the fridge at the same time as Kat slams the door shut from the outside and locks it.

Chets struggles. He starts pulling his head back and making that god-awful gurgling sound. But Mak and I are prepared. We swapped our shorts for trousers and put hoodies over our T-shirts. Our hoods are up and pulled tightly around our faces so that only are eyes are exposed. There isn't much of a target for Chets to spit at.

He thrashes around but we hold tight and let the cold work its way into him. Within a few minutes I feel him weaken.

'I'm really sorry about this, Chets,' I say, as we use our backpack straps to tie his hands together and to a metal shelving unit. And then I tie a tea towel around his mouth.

I think he's glaring at me but it's hard to tell with those hunter's eyes.

'That went well,' Mak says.

'I knock on the inside of the fridge door and call through. 'We're OK, Kat. Chets is tied up and, err, incapacitated. Keep a lookout and we'll holler when we're ready.'

'Well done, guys,' she calls back. 'And say hi to Chets for me.'

'Katja says hi,' I say, turning to Chets.

He makes a noise in his throat that sounds somewhere between a growl and 'I'm going to kill you in the face'.

'Chets says hi back,' I call.

'Let's get started,' Mak says, looking like he's thinking what I'm thinking. This bit is not going to be fun.

''K. You're stronger,' I say. 'You hold him and I'll … you know.'

Chets looks from me to Mak and back again. I think he's scared. Which, to be fair, he should be, cos we're basically about to torture him.

Mak steps behind him and grabs Chets' head. He fights. Tries to wriggle out of Mak's grasp. But we don't call Mak 'Big Mak' for nothing. He's strong –

much stronger than Chets. And Chets' extra super-alien powers are being counterbalanced by the cold.

I rip the tea towel from Chets' face and, before he can speak or spit, I ram a handful of moss into his mouth. I do it fast, so I don't have to see those black pincers, and then I tie the tea towel back. 'Really sorry, Chets.'

He chokes and splutters. I think for a moment we might have to take the gag off and perform the Heimlich manoeuvre.

'Just swallow,' I say. 'It will be much better if you swallow.'

I look at Mak and can see he's struggling with this too. I'm glad Kat's not in here – she wouldn't be able to handle it. She gets tears in her eyes when she accidentally steps on a snail.

Chets swallows and retches like he's going to be sick. Then he stops. Slumps to the ground. Not asleep but in a kind of daze.

'This is the worst thing I've ever done,' I say.

'Same, mate.' Mak pulls his hood down. Even though the fridge is super cold, he's sweating. I realise I am too. 'What next?' he says.

'I guess we wait.'

We sit in silence, keeping watch over Chets.

Neither of us says it, but I know we're both terrified that we've killed him or something. Maybe the moss is poisonous to humans. Maybe once someone has bugged out, there's no going back.

Now that he's still, I can look at him more closely and I realise that the changes I thought I saw from a distance are real. Chets is taller. Not a lot, but enough for it to be noticeable. And obviously there's the whole eye thing. But there's also something odd about his skin – it's starting to flake and peel. And I don't think it's sunburn.

He suddenly twitches, taking us by surprise. I think he's going to attack us, but it's as if he doesn't know we're there. He writhes around like his whole body is unbearably itchy and he can't scratch it away. Then he starts to choke.

'Get the towel off,' I say and me and Mak work together to loosen the knot, pull it away from his face and tip him forward. Chets is still choking and his face is turning a funny colour. And not funny in a good way, or a waspy way, funny in a close-to-death way. Mak thumps him hard on his back. Something flies out of his mouth and pings off the wall on the other side of the room.

'That didn't look like a spitball,' Mak says.

I run over to the wall and crouch down to examine the missile. 'It's one of his mouth pincers,' I say.

'Is that a good thing?' Mak asks.

'It's either a good thing or he's about to die,' I say, and panic rushes through my body. 'Chets,' I shake him gently. 'Snap out of it, buddy. Talk to me.'

'Look at his eyes.' Mak's jiggling around with excitement.

The dark centres of Chets' eyes are lightening from metallic black to a deep brown. The angry yellow rings are fading.

'Chets, are you back?' I say, feeling that pinch inside my nose that means I might start crying.

'Lance?' Chets says, finally focusing his eyes on me. The sight of those chocolate browns looking at me is too much and a tear leaks from my eye.

'It's been ages – what's happening?' Kat yells through the door.

'Hey, Katja,' Chets calls out. 'Basically, I ate some magic moss and it made me feel a bit weird, but the good news is that I don't think I'm a sporeling anymore.'

'Yay!' Kat calls. 'Can I open the door then?'

'I think it's safe,' I say and I can't stop smiling.

20
The New Chets

With Chets back in the group, our confidence is rising. It seems like his alien transformation hadn't gone far enough to cause any permanent damage. He coughed up the other pincer, and where his skin was peeling, I can see new, pinkish-brown human skin underneath.

We're making our way back to my room to collect the rest of the moss, which we need for the next stage of our plan.

'Hhhhccchhh,' Chets says, for the twentieth time. 'Hhhhhhhcccccchhhhhh.'

'I don't think it works anymore, Chets,' Kat says. 'Which is a good thing, right?'

'I don't know. I didn't like the pincers, but the balls of venom were kind of cool. Imagine what I could do with them – send anyone to sleep whenever I wanted.'

'The spitballs were gross, man,' Mak says. 'I can't believe you want them back.'

'Yeah, the Chets we knew would be disgusted,' I say, looking across at my best friend, who has a new air of something about him.

'Turning into an alien changes you, literally and also emotionally,' he says.

We all laugh. It's so good to have him back.

'I'm sorry for the things I said to you, Lance,' he says. 'You're my best friend and you've always had my back.'

Deep breaths. 'I can explain why I trapped Trent in the toilets, and why I didn't tell you about it.'

'I know you did it for a good reason,' Chets says. 'You don't need to explain. Let's talk about it once we're out of this flipping crater.'

'Oh my gosh, Chets said an almost-swear,' Kat gasps. 'You really have changed!'

'Welcome to the new me,' Chets smiles and starts trying to walk with what I think is supposed to be a gangster swagger.

'Chets,' I say, 'you're a straight savage.'

All is quiet in the dorm corridor. We tiptoe down the steps to my room and quietly open the door, expecting to find Trent sleeping with the CPAP on again. But he's not there.

'That's weird,' says Kat. 'I would have thought Trent would be too scared to go out on his own.'

'I wonder if he got caught?' Mak walks over to the bed and checks underneath it, just in case.

'There's no sign of a struggle,' I say. 'And if the bug-eyes knew he was here, they'd be waiting for us too.'

'So where is he then?' says Chets.

We look around the room, all of us blank. And that's when I realise something else is missing, too.

'Guys, the bag of moss,' I say. 'It's not here.'

'The CPAP is missing too,' says Mak.

Mak and Kat start opening the drawers and checking under the duvet, but I know where it's gone.

'Trent's taken them,' I say. 'He's taken them and gone for the gate, to try to escape.'

'He's saving himself,' Kat gasps.

'Of course he is,' says Mak. 'Why the hell did we trust him?'

This is bad. Really bad. We can't run the plan without the tardigrades.

'Can we get some more?' Chets asks.

'We took all of it,' Kat says. 'There was nothing

left at the gate, and all the rest got dug up when they made the ditch.'

'The ditch runs all the way around the crater,' says Chets. 'Except for by the road and...'

A noise from outside the door makes us jump. The door handle turns – someone's coming in to the room. I look around. There's nowhere to hide, no way to escape, no weapons to hand.

'Brace yourselves, guys,' I whisper. 'We'll need to bundle in together... One...'

The door starts to open.

'Two...'

I see a hand, and a shoe.

'Three!' I yell, and we all jump on the person coming in.

'Get off! It's me!' a familiar voice shrieks at us.

'Ade!' Kat says, and her death grip/headlock becomes a tight hug.

'You made it! I knew you'd make it.' Mak is grinning like a mad person.

I'm so happy, I can't say anything. She's dirty, has a few scratches and scrapes and a torn T-shirt sleeve. But she's OK. She was right – she was more than capable. I should have trusted her.

'Good to see you, Chets,' says Adrianne.

'Good to see you too.' Chets hugs her.

'So where are we with the plan?' she asks, once we've all calmed down a bit.

'It was going great,' I say. 'As you can see from Chets' lack of creepy pincers and alien eyes. But…'

'Trent did a runner with the tardimoss,' Mak says.

'What a swine,' Adrianne says. 'Not that I'm shocked.'

'I always thought you liked Trent,' Chets says, looking a bit confused.

In spite of the really, really bad situation we're in, we all start to laugh.

'What?' says Chets.

'I'll tell you later,' Ade says, taking off her backpack. 'But first, you might want to take a look at what I've got in here.'

She unzips her bag. It's crammed full of slimy green moss.

'How?' Kat says.

'I went to the river to try to lose the bug-eyes,' says Ade. 'And there was lots of it there. I thought I might as well grab some.'

'Legend,' I say. 'We're back in business.'

It's 6.30pm when we slink through the centre, back to our old friend the kitchen. Thanks to Chets' inside information, we know that the bug-eyes will eat dinner at exactly 7pm. And we worked out for ourselves what they'll be eating.

The kitchen is lined with shelves full of giant tubs and packets of different foods. We find the shelf we need, and look at our options.

'They've already had tomato, chicken and leek and potato,' I say.

'They'll want something different to keep a balanced nutritional content,' says Chets. 'So there's lentil, chunky mushroom, or farmhouse vegetable.'

'We'll be able to disguise it best in the farmhouse vegetable,' I say. 'Look at all the lumps of green in there – there's no way they'll notice some handfuls of moss.'

'Good call,' says Mak, and he starts pushing all the other flavours of soup to the higher shelves, while the rest of us open the tubs of farmhouse vegetable and crumble in the moss. We give the soup a good stir, put the lids back on and by the time we're finished, you can't tell that the soup has been tampered with. We place the moss soup right at the front of the shelf that's easiest to access.

'How are we going to make sure they eat it?' Kat says.

'Leave that to me.' Chets pulls his Crater Lake sunglasses out of his pocket. 'The rest of you should hide – they'll be here any minute.'

Ade, Kat, Mak and I take refuge in our trusty safehouse, aka the fridge, leaving Chets to work his undercover magic.

'Are you sure Chets is up to this?' Mak whispers.

'He can do it,' I say.

'Oh, look, it's Mr Tomkins,' Kat says, as the kitchen door opens and two bug-eye workers walk in.

The four of us peek very carefully through the tiny opening we've left so we can spy out of the fridge.

'He's ruined his special T-shirt. He's going to be really upset about that when all this is over,' says Adrianne.

'RIP T-shirt,' I say. 'It's the end of an era. Life will never be the same again.'

'And there's Khalil,' says Mak. 'Mr Tomkins and Khalil, hanging out together, making some soup.'

'At last,' Chets says to them, as they walk across the kitchen. 'I've been hunting excessively all day. My body needs sustenance.'

'Proper nourishment is vital to these soft bodies,' Mr Tomkins says. 'We will prepare the food with all due haste.'

'Good,' says Chets. 'I shall help you to prepare the nourishment.' He picks a tub of farmhouse vegetable off the shelf and passes it to Khalil.

'We are grateful for your assistance, Hunter. But should you not return to your duties? The human prey is still loose in the crater. We cannot allow them to hinder us.'

'I am the hunter, and I will decide the best use of my time.' Chets thumps his fist down on the counter in an aggressive way that I didn't think Chets was capable of.

'Of course, Hunter. As you wish,' Mr Tomkins says, and he starts pouring the mossy surprise into a huge pot on the cooker.

'When the nourishment is hot, serve it immediately,' Chets says. 'I will perform one more circuit of the crater before I join the hive for my sustenance.' He walks out of the kitchen.

Mr Tomkins and Khalil finish warming the

soup, then they carry it from the kitchen in the steaming pot.

'You don't think the water bears have been cooked to death, do you?' Kat says.

'They should be fine – remember they can survive extreme conditions, including really hot or cold. They're probably swimming around in that soup having a tardi-party,' says Mak.

'Did you see me?' Chets comes running in. 'How awesome was I?'

'You were so convincing,' says Adrianne. 'I've never heard you speak that way before. It was weird.'

'You did great, Chets,' I say, 'but it's going to be harder to convince Hoche and Digger you're still a bug-eye. Are you ready for this?'

'I'm ready,' he says.

'Then let's prepare for the final stage,' I say. 'It's all or nothing now.'

21
The Ticking Clock

We sit in a clearing behind the centre to go through the endgame. Each of us has a role to play, and if any of us fail, the whole plan will come crashing down. It requires total investment from all of us, and total investment is challenging when you haven't slept properly in two days.

Everyone is assigned a job to match their skillset.

'Big Mak: you understand construction and you're strong. You'll be stationed at the dam site. Your priority will be getting that dam down, however you can. We need the river flowing back down into the crater. Ade: you're smart and you're fast. I need you to help Mak at the dam. You'll need to distract the guards while he susses out where the weak spot is. Once he's made a dent in it, I want you both to attack a bug-eye. The rest of the plan depends on them releasing that pheromone and drawing all the others up to the river. Use the swarm. They'll be frenzied and aggressive, so you might even be able to get them to do a lot of the dam destruction for you. Try to lure them into the riverbed so that when the dam breaks, they're swept away.

'We'll get it done,' Mak says.

'And keep each other safe. When the river floods through, you both need to be clear of the torrent.'

'Affirmative,' Adrianne nods.

'Ah, Big Mak and Adrianne – the perfect team,' Kat says. 'Your ship name can be Big Mad. No, Marianne. No – Madriak!'

Both Mak and Adrianne turn pink, so I move on.

'Chets, they don't know you're not a bug-eye anymore. You can be our undercover brother. You need to keep Digger and Hoche from going with the others when they swarm. They're clever – they'll work out what we're trying to do and that could jeopardise the whole thing. We need to keep them away from the dam.'

'Got it,' Chets says.

'Katja: you're blessed with an innocent face and mad climbing skills. I need you to lure Digger.'

'No problem,' she smiles.

'And I'll take on Hoche. She'll come for me anyway. It's about time we faced off.'

The sun is getting low in the sky and we need that dam down before it gets dark. The bug-eyes can see at night, and we can't, so they'll have too much of an advantage if we leave it late.

'Good luck, everyone,' I say. 'Let's get ready to rumble.'

I wait nervously with Katja in the trees at the side of the lawn.

'I hope Madriak are alright,' Kat says.

'They're a couple of bad-As,' I say. 'And they'll look out for each other. I'm sure they're OK.'

'I guess we'll find out soon, one way or another.'

It's still wicked hot, but for the first time in days there's a slight breeze. It feels amazing as it tickles my skin, and it carries the faint smell of blossom. It's almost like life is coming back into the crater. It gives me hope.

'Look!' Kat says, pointing at the bug-eyes who up until now have been completely engrossed in draining the lake. The water is ankle-deep. Like a flock of frightened deer, they all suddenly raise their heads and sniff the air. They turn in the direction of the dam, and then they drop their tools and run.

'Oh gosh, how are Ade and Mak going to manage all those angry bug-eyes?' Kat says.

'We can't worry about that now,' I say. 'Besides, the force is strong with them. If anyone can do it, they can. Look – Chets is up.'

Chets has been stalking around the treeline, as if he's on hunter duty. When the bug-eyes start to swarm, he runs towards Hoche and Digger.

'Hunters, cease!' he calls, as they turn to join the others flocking to the dam site.

'He's totally got the bug-eye lingo down,' I say.

'Yeah, he's embracing the role.'

Hoche and Digger turn to Chets, who is still wearing his sunglasses. That's our sign to take position. Kat turns and hugs me.

We leave the shelter of the trees and sprint on to the floodlit lawn. The white lights glare down on us, like spotlights. We're out in the open and visible to everyone in the crater. My vision blurs, so I can't see anybody except Kat, and this is where we go our separate ways. She's gone in a swoosh of colour, and I run, as fast as I can, towards the patch of tall trees on the far side of the lawn. In the corner of my eye I see the distorted shapes of Chets, Hoche and Digger. Chets starts to jog my way. Digger gallops after Kat. Hoche is shooting towards me like an arrow with a vendetta.

I close my mind to everything around me except the enormous tree looming ahead, and making my legs move faster and faster. I expect every moment to be tackled from behind, flung into the hard dirt ground, my teeth clashing together, the breath being knocked from my body, but Chets must be doing a good job of slowing Hoche down. I reach the tree. It has a rope ladder on one side. I launch myself at it and grab the highest rung I can, then I start to pull myself up, my muscles throbbing. I'm not the best at climbing and I wouldn't usually attempt this without a harness, but I have to get higher.

I'm a third of the way up when Hoche reaches the tree. I look down to see her lurching at me, but her fingers miss my foot by a few centimetres. 'I've got you now, Lance,' she says. 'This is a dead end – there's nowhere left for you to run.'

I keep moving upwards, one rung at a time,

until I reach the wooden platform. Once I've heaved myself on to it, I look down. Hoche and Chets are still on the ground, having a discussion. Chets points to a tree nearby and jogs towards it, while Hoche starts to climb up after me.

When I look down, all I can see are those creepy-mad eyes: the shiny black and glowing yellow. The urge to jump is almost overwhelming, but I know I have to wait.

I look across the lawn to the climbing wall. Katja is halfway up it, taking a complicated route – zig-zagging across it like a rainbow-coloured ant. Every now and then, she stops to pour something on the hand and footholds. She's totally doing it like a boss.

Digger is behind her but not as fast as I'd have thought he'd be. He's definitely changed shape. He's bigger, especially across his chest, so he must be stronger, but he's sort of twitching in a pretty disturbing way. He reaches the wall and throws himself on to it like an animal. He goes for the direct route upwards, grabbing the handholds and perching on the tiny footholds like he's done this a million times. Every now and then he stops and his whole body sort of shudders.

Hoche looks over and smiles. 'Ah, the sporeling's metamorphosis is complete. Take a look, Lance, at the majestic form of a hunter.'

I watch in horror as Digger's shuddering grows more and more violent. Then the top of his back massively expands, bursting through his polo shirt, which falls in shreds to the floor. His shoulder blades are overly prominent, and still growing. They pull apart, splitting his skin open to reveal a mass of dark grey fuzz underneath. He claws at his face and his human skin just peels away exposing his new skin, which is matte black, like velvet. He doesn't look like a person anymore. He doesn't look like a giant wasp, or one of those huge-eyed aliens you see on TV. He's something I could never have imagined. Some impossible monster with a mix of human and insect-like features and a head like a mouldy potato. Although Digger's head was a bit potatoey before he transformed, so maybe that's just him. And, just as I think he couldn't get any scarier, his shoulder blades extend out of his back, dripping black goo, and start to stretch into what can only be wings.

Katja screams, and I don't blame her. I want to

scream and I'm not up close and personal with the Digger monstrosity.

'He'll have her soon,' Hoche says and carries on climbing up my tree.

I watch Kat with my heart racing and my mouth dry. She's almost at the top of the wall. He's close behind, but he's having trouble moving his hands and feet. Our plan is working. Kat's fingers grasp the summit and she starts to heave herself up. Digger tries to follow, but he can't move his right hand from the handhold. His feet are stuck too. He jiggles about, and pulls and pulls, and finally gets his left hand loose. He lunges towards Katja and grabs her shoe. For half a second she falls back, then she drops something on Digger and kicks out. Digger makes a noise that's somewhere between a scream and a roar. His wings stop unfurling – they must be stuck, too. Katja clings to the wall, and slowly eases herself up, leaving her trainer in Digger's hand, and Digger roaring in fury, stuck to the superglued wall like a paralysed spider.

'Doesn't look like he's going to have her after all,' I say, so full of relief that I feel like I might wet my pants.

Hoche looks over. 'No. No, no, no. This is your doing, Lance Sparshott, you vile little reprobate.' She quickens her pace. Time to move.

I ease myself around the platform to the other side of the trunk where a thick rope is swinging slightly in the breeze. The leap of faith. An uncomfortably large distance away, stretched between two trees, is a large net. So there's me on my ridiculously high platform and then a load of empty space, which I have to cross if I'm going to get away from Hoche and put her out of action.

I turn to see her fingertips appear at the edge of the platform. I hold the rope and try not to think about the huge drop to the ground. If I fall, there's no way I'm going to make it without breaking most of the bones in my body.

The top of her head appears, and those truly awful eyes. She hisses at me, which I think is alien-speak for 'I hate you and I'm going to kill you-slash-use your body as a host for my parasitic sporelings.'

I count three breaths. I hear the click of her heel on the wooden ledge. Then I fling myself from the platform.

At first I freefall – down through the air with

nothing to hold me back. The feeling is sickening. I brace myself for the kick when the rope I'm clinging to for dear life goes taut. This is the most dangerous moment – the part where I'm most likely to lose my grip and fall. The rope jerks, my hands slip. My body jars at the bounce. I try to grasp the rope tighter, but it slides through my hands, burning my palms. The forward momentum is still swinging me towards the net. I just need to hold on for a second longer. My sore hands reach the end of the rope, as I near the landing net. I have one chance. So I let go and basically fly through the last bit of empty air and crash face first into the net. I manage to grab it with one hand and I try to lock it shut while the rest of my body bounces away from the net and then back towards it again. I get my other hand on to a rope, then a foot. I've made it. I hang there for a second, dripping with sweat and relief. There's no breath left in my body.

But Hoche has grabbed the swinging rope and is strapping herself into the safety harness.

I force myself onwards, climbing the net as quickly as I can, though my whole body wants to give up and die. I only have a few seconds before she jumps.

I slide clumsily on to the platform – I'm not going to be winning any awards for being slick – then I take off my backpack and pull out the can of olive oil.

Hoche jumps at the same moment she clocks the oil. She howls, but it's too late. I pour it all over the safety net.

When she hits it, she tries to grab on, but her hands just slip off. She bounces back and tries again on the return swing, but her hands are oily now so she has even less success. She's losing momentum and she can't get on to the net. She's stuck and she knows it.

She scream-roars – scroars – like Digger did, only hers is higher pitched so it sounds even more terrible. I put my hands over my ears while I grin at her furious face. The rope is almost out of swing, so she's just dangling from the harness in the centre point between the trees. She can't get to either side and she can't drop down. One of her shoes falls off into the darkness below.

'You'll pay for this,' she says. 'It doesn't matter what happens to me. My race is stronger, smarter and better than you in every way. We will dominate this world and you will be forgotten.'

'I'd love to stop and chat, Miss,' I say. 'But if you look to your left, you'll see that the river is flowing back into Crater Lake, so I'm afraid your precious sporelings aren't going to be escaping any time soon.'

She turns to see the river surging down to the bottom of the crater, carrying most of the bug-eye workers with it. They're so weak from the moss-soup and the cold water that they're not even attempting to climb out, just scrabbling around with panicked looks on their faces. Mak and Adrianne did it.

I climb down from the tree and collapse on the floor.

'How's the tunnel blocking going?' I ask Kat, who runs over and flops down beside me.

'Chets is nearly finished. He worked out how to operate the digging machinery,' she says.

'So he's digging in reverse?'

'Yes, and still wearing the sunglasses. He thinks they make him look swag.' She smiles. 'Well done, Lance. Your plan worked.'

'It was all of us,' I say. 'That was some epic climbing.'

'I nearly fell when that black slime started oozing out of him.' She looks over to where the thing that used to be Digger is glued to the wall, jerking around still trying to get loose. 'Poor Digger – he looks disgusting.'

'An abomination,' I agree.

'I guess he must have skipped dinner, or maybe because he's been turned the longest the moss didn't work so well on him. Do you think if we give him some more water bears he might turn back?'

'I don't think there's any coming back from that,' I say. 'But hopefully the others will be OK. Are you up to doing one more job?'

'Of course.'

'We're not safe until we get the word out. Will you take my mobile and climb up to the roof? If you can get reception, phone the police, MI5, the Men in Black and my mum.'

'I'm on it,' she says, taking my mobile and running back across the lawn.

I want nothing more than to lie here and fall asleep, but there's still work to be done, so I force myself to get up.

Without my phone, I'm not sure what time it is exactly, but the crescent moon is high in the sky, and the stars are twinkling. With the floodlights on I can see the lawn and the lake, and they're buzzing with activity.

I walk over to where Chets is driving the digger, and obviously having the time of his life. He grins at me and gives me a thumbs up.

'When you're done,' I call, dodging out of the way as a pile of earth tumbles out of the scoop, 'can you go and look for Digger's keys? If we can get into his office, we might be able to use the phone. I don't know if Kat's gonna have any luck getting reception.'

'He usually keeps them in his pocket,' he yells.

'I think his trousers are still mostly intact,' I say, 'though I don't even want to think about what he looks like underneath. The keys might have fallen out when he turned.'

'If not, I'll climb up and see if I can get them,' Chets says.

'You sure you're OK with that? He looks pretty scary.'

'Don't worry, I can handle it.'

I give him a wave and make my way to the lake. It's going to take a while to get used to this new Chetan.

The lake is full of bug-eyes splashing about. Adrianne and Big Mak are running around the edges, poking them back in with oars when they get too close to dry land.

'Hey, Lance!' Big Mak shouts. 'We did it!'

'Woohoo!' Adrianne punches the air.

'You guys did amazing,' I yell. 'You're heroes!'

'You too, mate.' Big Mak comes running over to me. 'Some of this lot are turning human, so we can start getting them out.'

'They're tired, though. Maybe we could get something to help them, some life-jackets or something?' Adrianne prods Atul, who definitely still has bug-eyes, deeper into the water.

'I think there's a dinghy in the boat shed,' I say. 'I saw it when we were hiding in there.'

'That would be perfect.'

'I'll go get it.' I run around the lake to the pier side, open the door to the boat shed and flick on the light.

I see what I need towards the back of the shed – behind the canoes and oars there are some inflatable rafts. It's going to be a squeeze to get to them, so I take off my backpack and chuck it on to the pier, then I go for the inflatables, climbing over piles of ropes and oars until I'm at the back of the shed.

Suddenly, the light flickers. My first thought is that the lightbulb must have popped, but I turn on instinct and, in the last flash of light, I see her. Then everything goes black. I crouch down behind the rafts.

'It's no good hiding,' Hoche's voice hisses from somewhere in the darkness. 'I can see you.'

I swallow. Damn those bug-eyes.

'Miss Hoche,' I say, 'I thought I left you hanging out by the leap of faith. Get it? Hanging out?'

She doesn't laugh. 'I managed to find my way out of your pathetic trap. Anger is a great motivator.' Her voice is a little closer this time. 'You should know – a boy like you, full of anger and aggression. If you were going to make it past today, you'd only end up in prison.'

'You've got me all wrong,' I say, fumbling with the inflatables in front of me. 'The things I've done – trapping Trent in the toilets, everything at Crater Lake – I didn't do them out of anger. I did them to help my friends.'

'And now you've ruined our plans,' she says. She must be barely more than a metre away now. 'My sporelings are destroyed. Soon I'll be the only one left.'

'You don't like soup?' I say.

'My human body is allergic to carrots. So I found alternative nourishment.'

'OK,' I say. I'm stalling. I need a few seconds more. 'Firstly, a carrot allergy? That's random. And, secondly, the way you say "alternative nourishment" sounds totally creepy, like you were eating human entrails or something.'

'I know what you're doing,' she says. She's so close I can feel her breath on my arm. 'But there's no way of getting out of this alive. You're not clever enough to defeat me.'

'See, that's where you're wrong,' I say, and I yank the ripcord on the dinghy in front of me. It pops up hard and starts inflating, knocking Hoche back. I hear a crash and a scroar and I run, clambering over the boats towards the light coming in around the edge of the door. I fling it open and run out on to the pier, grabbing my backpack.

There's a deafening scroar behind me, and Hoche comes running out of the shed.

'Do you know what, Miss?' I say, running and

trying to open my backpack. 'I might not be in the top group for maths. I might not be on the football team. I might not have the most house points. But that doesn't mean I don't have smarts and it doesn't mean I don't have skills.'

I'm at the end of the pier now. I could jump into the lake, but that isn't going to get this finished.

Hoche slows down to a walk. She knows I'm not going anywhere.

'Compared to me, you're nothing, Lance Sparshott. It's like that ridiculous game you all play – the one with the Geek, the Robot and the Overlord. I'm the Overlord and I was put here to enslave geeks like you.'

'You're wrong,' I say.

'You're pointless and weak – the archetypal geek.'

'Hell, yes, I'm the geek and proud of it,' I say, taking one more step back. 'I meant you're wrong about you.'

She tried to step toward me, but her stupid heel is caught in between the wooden boards of the pier. She wobbles.

'You're not the Overlord, you're the Robot.'

I launch myself at her, and as she opens her

mouth to scroar, I stuff in a bunch of moss and hold my hand over her mouth, pushing us both over the edge of the pier. She fights me as we fall, but as we plunge into the water, the shock of the cold makes her gasp. She swallows the moss. I let go of her face and hope I never have to get that close to a teacher again, then I leave her to splutter back to the surface.

I take a breath and swim for the shore.

22
Facing the Future

I knew when I went on the trip to Crater Lake that I was going to be homesick, but I didn't realise how much.

It's 8.37am. (I know that cos I got my phone back.) And I'm sitting on the sofa in the snug room at my house.

Katja and Chets both managed to call for help, and not long after my final showdown with Hoche, the police showed up, followed by ambulances, some official-looking guys in suits and all of our parents. They'd found Trent not far from the activity centre, crying on a tree stump. He'd used up all the oxygen, run out of snacks and got lost in the woods. They asked us some questions while we were there, and then let us go home to rest.

I've sat here a million times – this is my favourite room in the house. But this time, it's different.

'I can't believe you kept this house hidden from us all this time,' Chets says. 'It's like a mansion.'

'And there was everyone thinking you were a tramp from the wrong side of the tracks.' Mak shoves a whole burger into his mouth.

'I never said we were poor,' I say, and dunk a chip in some ketchup.

'Well, now we can come here every weekend.' Katja is lying at the other end of my sofa, yawning like she hasn't slept for, well, two days and two nights. 'You'll still come, won't you, Ade and Chets? Even though you're going to Bing with the genius kids.'

'I'm not going to Bing,' Ade says.

'What?' Mak nearly chokes on his burger.

'I never said I was going there. It's not for me. I'm going to Latham with you guys.'

We all stare at her in surprise.

'It's like I told you at Crater Lake,' she says. 'People are always making assumptions.'

Our parents are all in the kitchen having some kind of crisis meeting, so we eat and chat and laugh together, until the tiredness starts to catch up with us.

Katja falls asleep first, curled up like a kitten.

Then Mak just passes out on the floor, with a pillow under his head. I guess he's used to sleeping rough, so our carpet is probably pretty comfortable in comparison.

Adrianne lies on the other sofa, her face turned away, just like she slept with my CPAP at the centre.

'You're never coming to Bing, are you, Lance?' Chets says.

'No. I'd never get in there, and I'd hate it if I did.'

'How will I get by without you?'

'Chets,' I say, looking over to where he's made himself a nest on the floor. 'Think about what you've been through over the past few days. You're going to be just fine.' And I believe that – I honestly do.

'I don't think Trent's going to mess with me anymore,' he says.

'No chance. You were a bad-A.'

'I was, wasn't I?' He's grinning bigger and bolder than I've ever seen him grin before. 'We'll still be friends, though, right?'

'Wherever we go, whatever we do, even if we don't see each other for ages, I promise you that you will always, always be my friend.'

'You too,' he says. 'My best friend. Night, Lance.' And he lets his head fall onto the pillow.

Within two minutes, he's snoring gently, like a bear cub.

My eyes are so heavy, and my head is full of thoughts and feelings. I look around at my friends and wonder why I didn't let them in sooner. Crater Lake has changed my life, in so many ways. And I know that no matter what lies ahead, I'll deal with it. Actually, we'll deal with it together.

I turn on the CPAP and strap the mask to my face, listening to the comforting soft whirr of its pumps filling the tube with oxygen. Then I let my eyelids drop, and in a safe and happy place, with a full stomach and the people I love around me, I snuggle into a warm haze of contentment, and finally go to sleep.

Acknowledgements

Firstly, I would like to thank everyone at Firefly: Penny, Meg, Simone, Janet and Rebecca. To be a Firefly is to be part of a close team, and I know how hard-working and passionate you all are about every Firefly book and author. Thanks to Anne Glenn for a cover that I make heart-eyes at every time I look at it, and to Fritha, publicist extraordinaire. Thank you to my agent, Kirsty, who guides me with such wisdom and kindness – I couldn't manage without you. Thanks to all my author friends who have reached out and offered a word of advice, encouraging message, or cheering cup of tea when I've needed it. These things make such a difference and I hope to return the kindness one day, if I haven't already. To wonderful Lorraine, Eloise, Ness and BB, who are always at the end of a DM to help me fight another day. To Vashti who read this story before anyone else, and gave me the confidence to share it.

Thank you to the teachers who have embraced my books and me (sometimes in actual hug form):

the Liverpool lot (Ashley Booth, Ian Hunt, Laura Baxter, and Les Hall); Bruce McInnes, Jane Clapp, Maaria Khan, Neil Black, Matthew Girvan, Karl Duke, Dean Boddington (told you I'd put you in my book), Laura Reid, Tami Wylie, Sophie Topliss, and my wonderful friends Ann Hopson and Simon Hawley. There are SO MANY other teachers and TAs who I'm grateful to, and I'm sorry that I can't add all of your names. Please know that every kindness you've shown is appreciated from the bottom of my heart.

Thanks to the brilliant bloggers who are so committed to sharing their love of reading, especially BookLoverJo Clarke, LibraryGirl&BookBoy Jo, GoldenBooksGirl Amy, everyone at @MyBookCorner, and bookwormhole Liam – your continued support is worth heaps. Thank you to the tireless booksellers who I know shout about my books as often and loudly as they can, especially Karen at Waterstones Cirencester, Bronnie at BookWagon, and the bunch of much-missed misfits formerly of Waterstones Uxbridge, but temporarily scattered – Jane, Phoenix, Tom, Heather, Alex, and even Lance.

And finally, thank you to the people who keep me going on a daily basis, through their love and unwavering support: my family – Mum, Dad, Julie and Alfie; my friends Nic, Laura, Emma, and Sarah; my children – Stanley, Teddy, Mia, Helena and Luis (I was going to be mean and put your nicknames here but decided that some of you wouldn't see the funny side); and my husband Dean, who thinks I should just be writing here that it's ALL because of him. I love you all so much.

And, of course, to my readers! Thank you for turning the pages of my stories, for laughing with my characters, and gasping at the twisty bits. I hope Crater Lake takes you on an adventure that you won't forget.

Crater Lake: Evolution

Just when you thought it was safe to go back to sleep…

It's five months since the nightmare Year Six school trip to Crater Lake and Lance and his friends have started at their new schools. But something has gone very wrong in their hometown of Straybridge. There's been an explosion at the university, a mysterious test creature is apparently on the loose, and no one is allowed in or out of town until it's recaptured. On top of this, Lance suddenly notices something weird about his mum's behaviour…

Suspicious of recent incidents, Lance sets out to reunite his scattered team. But things are worse than he feared. Cut off from help, Lance, Kat, Mak, Ade, Chets and new friend Karim, are going to have to think bigger and bolder to save their families.

And there's something else out there – something straight from their nightmares…

May 2021, £7.99 from Firefly Press
ISBN 978-1-913102-64-7

Firefly

www.fireflypress.co.uk